Sabo

Sabotage Flight

by

Paul Meyerhoff II

Illustrations by Steve Hillyer

DIMI PRESS
Salem, Oregon

DIMI PRESS
3820 Oak Hollow Lane, SE
Salem, Oregon 97302
© 1995 by Paul Meyerhoff II
Printed in the United States of America
First Edition

Library of Congress Cataloging-In-Publication Data:
    Meyerhoff, Paul, 1949-
        Sabotage flight / by Paul Meyerhoff II : illustrations by
    Steve Hillyer. -- 1st ed.
            p.   cm.
        Summary: Twelve-year-old Andy helps his father, a US
    Marshal and pilot with the Civil Air Patrol, investigate some
    mysterious activities involving foreigners stealing minerals off
    the Alaskan coast.
        ISBN: 0-931625-24-6 : $9.95
        [1. Air pilots--Fiction. 2. Fathers and sons--Fiction.
    3. Alaska--Fiction. 4. Mystery and detective stories.]
    I. Hillyer, Steve, ill. II. Title
    PZ7.M571755Sab   1995
    [Fic]--dc20   94-37177
                                                CIP
                                                 AC

*This is a work of fiction. The events described here are imaginary:
the characters are fictitious and not intended to represent living
persons:*

Cover design by Steve Hillyer and Bruce DeRoos
Edited by Sharon Thompson
Book design and lay-out by Marna Porath
Typeface 13 pt. Times

DEDICATION

FOR ANDERS
I love you, Bud.

Contents

1   Crow Pass, Alaska 1
2   Winner Creek 7
3   Mitchey Peters 17
4   The Town of Girdwood 25
5   Fixing the Cub 33
6   Kidnapped in Girdwood 41
7   Air Search 55
8   Virtual Reality 65
9   In the Cockpit 73
10   Recon 83
11   Debrief 105
12   Late Night in Seward 115
13   At the Seward Dock 121
14   Harbor Master's Office, Seward 129
15   A Plan of Action 137
16   Briefing at Girdwood 143
17   Montague Bay 151
18   Flight to Shore 159
19   Coast Guard Cutter Resolute 173

1
Crow Pass, Alaska

Climbing!" I hollered down to Dad.

"On belay!" he yelled back.

I could see him on the ground below me, about 25 feet down. His gray hair stuck out from underneath the red 49er's ball cap he had on. I chuckled knowing that he wore the cap because his hair was getting thin. If he didn't wear a cap, he complained, the top of his head got sunburned.

It was a cloudless summer day, and Dad and I had hiked up to Crow Pass, one of my favorite spots in the Chugach Mountains, to practice some rock climbing.

The Chugach Mountains stretch east from the city of Anchorage for about 150 miles and tower 8,500 feet above the glacial feed streams that criss-cross the base of the range. Over my shoulder was an unobstructed view of the tall snow-covered peaks and the glaciers, deep blue from thousands of years of ice accumulation, rimming the valley.

The rock face I was on was pretty technical. I had tried to climb it four or five times before, and it was always a challenge to get past the small, rock overhang that was just above my head. Sometimes I made it, and sometimes I couldn't hang on. But Dad said I did pretty well for a 12-year-old kid. I was glad to have him holding tension on the rope.

Just as I started climbing again, I heard the sounds of an airplane engine. It was sputtering and running very rough.

I yelled, "Dad! Do you hear that plane? It sounds like it's in trouble."

Down below Dad scanned the sky. He is tall, about six foot one, but he was standing among some rock boulders and he could not see clearly down the valley.

"I don't see it," he yelled. "Keep your eyes peeled, Andy. I'll keep holding tension on the rope."

I looked around to where I thought the sound was coming from just as a little plane flew into view up the canyon. It was flying near the waterfalls and was clearly in trouble.

"There it is! Up the valley!" I yelled. "It's coming this way!"

Dad looked over his shoulder. "I see it, Andy," he shouted. "Keep your eyes on it. Tell me where you think it's headed! It'll probably make an attempt at an emergency landing. If he does, he'll need help."

I knew what Dad was thinking. He's one of the few U.S. Marshals on active duty in Alaska and he is also a pilot. He'd be partly responsible for coordinating the ground search with the Civil Air Patrol if a plane went down. If we knew where the plane went into the forest, it would make the search much faster. If the pilot was injured, he would need our help as quickly as possible.

I focused my attention back to the plane. I didn't want to lose sight of it now.

The plane was descending out of the pass, and going down toward the valley floor below. We were at about the 1,500-foot level of the pass and the plane came right over our heads.

It was an old Piper Cub, all yellow with a black lightning bolt painted on the side. The wings were mounted on the top and the main wheels hung down from under the fuselage. The tail wheel was in the back, a "tail dragger," just like the one Dad flew at work.

"I don't recognize it. Do you?" I shouted.

Dad shook his head.

The engine wasn't developing enough power to keep the tiny plane flying. It was barely hanging in the air.

"He'll have to set her down pretty quickly," I yelled to Dad. "He doesn't have much altitude left."

"Keep your eyes on it, partner."

"I am."

The plane was so close, I could see the pilot but I couldn't make out any of his features. He had his head forward, probably looking for a place to land. There really was no safe place in Crow Pass and not much room for a small plane to maneuver, especially one with engine trouble.

The plane descended on down the narrow canyon toward the valley floor and Cook Inlet. I was praying to myself, "Come on engine, run strong. Come on." It didn't help. The plane just kept going down.

"Did you notice, Andy? No flaps," called Dad, talking about the slats on the back of the wing which are lowered to help slow the plane down for landing. "He'll have a hard time slowing her down. He'll have to get into the wind before he touches down."

"It didn't have tundra tires, either," I hollered. Those are the big, soft tires that make for easier landings on very rough terrain.

Dad shook his head. "He's going to be in for a pretty rough landing.

"Keep your eyes on him, Andy. About his only good landing spot will be in one of the clearings near the river." I thought Dad was really calm at this point, but then he rarely seemed to get very anxious.

"Is he going to crash?"

"If he's not gentle, and he turns her too steep, he'll lose too much altitude, and he'll risk a stall." A stall is when a plane stops flying, and noses over or spins toward the ground in what seems like an uncontrolled fashion. Near the ground, a stall is usually fatal. I'd seen Sean Tucker, the famous air show pilot, do amazing stalls in his little Pitts special biplane. Falling straight towards the ground, and then pulling it out at just the last second. But this wasn't an air show.

"I've lost sight of him," yelled Dad. "Do you still see it?"

"Got him in sight. He's going to set it down. He's turning up river—maybe he sees a gravel bar, or a patch of grass along Winner Creek," I called.

Dad nodded. "He's dropping below the trees. I see the spot! It's across from the Crow Creek Mine, up river about a mile or so from the old bridge."

The plane disappeared below the trees.

"Great job, Andy!" shouted Dad. "Let's get down there as quick as we can."

Dad carefully but rapidly lowered me to the ground. We grabbed our gear, and started loping down the trail to the Jeep.

2

Winner Creek

We reached the Jeep in record time. Dad had a radio on board and tried calling for help. But we were too far back in the mountains to raise anyone. Static was all that came back.

"No good," he said. "Andy, get your seat belt on. Then dig under the seat for the first-aid kit."

He roared out of the spot where we had parked. I barely got myself clipped in before we went around the first corner on the one-lane dirt road. I found the first-aid kit and held it on my lap as we bounced along.

"With luck, that pilot went down in one of the meadows on the other side of the creek from the mine," Dad said. "If I remember right, there is an old road of sorts that runs up along the river. The miners used it to haul in timber for their mines. Not much used anymore, but maybe we can get up it far enough to find the plane."

The road was about five miles down the Pass. Dad turned off and we were in old growth forest where the trees towered a hundred feet overhead. The ferns and devil's club grew six feet tall underneath. Without a trail or road, it was nearly impossible to get through the forest, mainly because of the alder bushes that seemed to grow sideways and always wanted to block every path. It was lucky we had the Jeep. With all the dead fallen trees and branches on the road, we never would have made it in a regular car.

Dad worked his way up the dirt road for a mile or so. "Look over there," he said, nodding to the left. "There's the old milling site for the mine." The mill buildings were all old and falling down. The tin roofs were rusting, and the wood structures seemed burned in places.

Before long the road descended down a steep embankment toward the river below. As we started down the hillside, I spotted the little plane at the far end of a clearing just up river.

"There it is!" I exclaimed.

Dad nodded.

Dad was cautious driving across the rocks and gravel. "If we wreck or get a flat, we aren't going to do that pilot much good," he said. But somehow he managed to keep his speed up and we reached the edge of the clearing after just a few more minutes. We drove up into a grassy meadow with really firm ground. The pilot was standing beside the plane looking inside the engine cowling.

"Are you okay?" Dad hollered as we reached the plane. The pilot turned around and looked up.

And he was a she—with long red hair! She was barely as tall as the top of the engine cowling, and she was wearing a long-sleeve shirt with a pair of blue jeans. A pair of gloves stuck out of her back pocket.

"Geez," she said. "My knees are still shaking like rubber bands."

Dad climbed out of the Jeep and walked over to her.

"You look like you're still shook up. Why don't you come over here and sit down for a few minutes. Have a drink of water. Sorry, water is the strongest stuff we have on board." Dad guided her over to the Jeep.

Up close she was really pretty. I guessed she was about 35 years old. Imprinted on her shirt pocket were the words "EAA - The Experimental Aircraft Association—Oshkosh." That's the sponsoring organization of the biggest, most famous fly-in in the country, the Oshkosh Air Show.

She pushed her sunglasses up and I could see the strain in her eyes. Then she flashed me a smile.

"Hi," she said.

"Hi," I said. That was all I could think of at the moment. I was embarrassed, but I didn't know why.

I moved over into Dad's seat and let her sit in my seat. I handed her a cup of water. She took a deep swallow and said, "Thanks." Then she smiled at me again, a wonderful smile that filled me with warmth.

"I'm. Marshal Armstrong. Sam Armstrong. This is my son, Andy.

"I'm Mitchey Peters. I'm from McCall, Idaho."

"Mitchey?" I said. "Isn't that a kind of unusual name?"

"It's really short for Michelle. My dad always called me Mitch. I liked Mitch okay, but my friends called me Mitchey, and I liked that the best."

"Oh," I said. She smiled.

"I sure was glad to see you drive up. How'd you get here so fast?"

"We were up the pass when you flew over about 20 minutes ago," said Dad. "We high-tailed it down here as fast as we could."

"That was a close call," he continued. "Are you sure you're okay?"

"I'm fine, really," she said. "Lucky for me that this clearing has such firm turf. I dead-sticked it in with room to spare."

"Well, you're still alive, and it looks like you have all your fingers and toes. Looks like your plane is okay, too," Dad said.

"Marshal Armstrong," she said. "Don't you fly a Super Cub sometimes?"

"Yeah, they let me out to fly it once in a while. Never often enough, though," Dad said. Dad was the chief law enforcement officer for one of the largest areas in Alaska, covering thousands of square miles. He supervised a bunch of people, and it never seemed to leave enough time for his love of flying. But he always seemed to have time for me.

"I've heard about you from friends of mine in McCall," she said.

"There's great flying and great skiing up there," he said. "What brings you to Alaska?"

"I'm spending the summer with my brother Pete in Fairbanks. I've always wanted to check out Alaska, and I thought Fairbanks would be a good place to go, especially since Pete offered me a place to stay. He's about the only person I know who lives up here," she said.

"How long have you been traveling?" Dad asked.

"I left McCall about a week ago and have been working my way north. I stopped last night in Valdez. It was raining," she said.

Dad and I eyed each other and laughed.

"What's so funny?" she asked.

"It almost always rains in Valdez," I said.

"So," Dad said, "do you have any idea what happened with your plane?"

"I'm not sure," said Mitchey. "The engine just suddenly started sputtering and coughing. Then it totally quit just before I had to land. That almost made me panic," she said.

"Well, why don't we have a look?" said Dad. "Andy—Bud, grab me a flashlight, will you?"

I reached over past Mitchey, and grabbed one of several flashlights in the glove box. I checked to make sure it was working, then hopped out of the Jeep. We walked over to the plane, and Dad started peering inside the cowling. I handed him the light like an assistant might hand a surgeon a scalpel. He looked up and smiled.

While Dad and Mitchey pored over the engine, I walked around the wing strut and peered into the old Cub, wanting to check out the cockpit. The back of that little plane was packed full of stuff! I could see cooking gear, a sleeping bag, camping junk, boxes of food, a fishing pole, a rifle, and even a hockey stick. I was amazed.

"Do you play hockey?" I asked Mitchey.

"When I was younger I loved to play hockey with the guys. I used to mix it up pretty good, too. Since I decided to fly to Alaska, I figured there would be frozen lakes and ice rinks everywhere. So I brought my skates and my stick, just in case!" she said.

"I play hockey, too!" I said. "I'll play any position but I like goalie the best. Dad said maybe this fall we'll buy a new set of goalie pads. Right, Dad?"

"Maybe for Christmas," he said absently, his head still buried under the cowling.

"Do you fly, too?" she asked me.

"Not solo yet, but I'm learning," I told her. "Dad's taught me some, and I read a lot about it.

And last spring I went to a week-long youth camp sponsored by the Federal Aviation Administration. It was part of the Young Eagles Learn-to-Fly program of the E.A.A. We spent days crawling over all kinds of aviation facilities."

"Sounds like you really like it," she said.

"Yeah, I do," I said. Suddenly I was shy again.

Dad pulled his head out from under the cowling. He had a serious look on his face, the professional one he wears at work.

"I think you should see this," he said to Mitchey.

I scrambled around the wing strut to see what was up. "What is it?" I asked.

"See these two leads here?" Dad said, showing us the wires. "They are connected to the magnetos which send energy to the engine's spark plugs. There are two leads because your plane has two sets of plugs for each cylinder," he explained to me.

"The leads normally are wrapped over here, out of the way of the exhaust manifold because the heat the manifold puts out is enough to melt them."

He straightened up.

"Someone has rewrapped the leads. See how they were wrapped around and are touching the exhaust manifolds? Now, I'm no airplane mechanic, but I'm willing to bet that these leads were wrapped like that intentionally to cause them to melt. That would cause you a total engine failure."

Mitchey was ashen. All the blood was gone from her face.

"Got any friends who don't want to hear from you again?" asked Dad.

3
Mitchey Peters

Mitchey looked at the burned wires.

"Who would do such a thing?" she asked.

"Good question," said Dad. "People don't mess with airplanes usually because it's a federal violation to tamper with one. That looks like an expert job, too," he said, waving his hand toward the wiring. "If you had crashed, the investigators for the National Transportation Safety Board might not have figured it out because the wiring probably would have melted in the fire after the crash anyway. Lucky for you that there was a clearing to land in."

"It couldn't have happened before I left McCall," said Mitchey. "Before I left, I had everything thoroughly checked by Mike Franklin at McCall Air Service. He's the best there is."

"I've heard of him," said Dad. "He used to be a member of the U.S. Ski Team. I saw him race a couple of times. He was a beautiful slalom racer, one of the world's best. He took over that air service from his dad, didn't he?"

Mitchey nodded. "About five years ago. He's one of the best bush pilots anywhere. You wouldn't believe where he can land a plane! I can't believe something like this would get by him."

"I've heard Mike is one of the safest pilots flying the Bitterroot country," said Dad.

"So," Dad said, "if no one you know wants you dead, and if your plane was checked out before you left McCall, what's happened along the way that might cause someone to want to eliminate you from this planet?"

"I have no idea," said Mitchey.

"Have you left the plane alone at all on your trip?"

"I've been camping along the Alaska Highway for most of the trip. Never really left the plane alone for more than an hour or two. I landed in

Whitehorse to refuel, and then flew south to Haines." She smiled at me. "I've heard so many wonderful stories about the bald eagles that nest in the canyons that I had to just stop there for awhile and look at those birds. I wanted to see them soaring. I must have seen twenty of them just west of that town.

"But most of the time I've been on the beaches or in the air. Since the weather was forecast to be pretty decent, I decided to fly up the coast line, past Cordova and into Valdez. When I got to Valdez the weather turned to absolute scud, and it really started pouring rain. After trying to sleep under the wing of the plane, I decided to treat myself to a hot shower and a real bed."

She stopped and thought.

"Valdez is the only place I really left the plane for a long time," she said finally.

Dad thought about that for a minute or two.

"We've been having some problems along the coast," Dad said. "Not quite sure what's going on, but maybe you saw something or someone you weren't supposed to see. Do you remember anything strange?"

Mitchey said, "Well, I don't know about anything strange or odd. I saw lots of neat things—fishing boats, and whales, and sea otters, and coastal glaciers. Even a few cruise-type ships."

"What do you mean, cruise-*type* ships?" Dad asked.

"You know, the kind that carry passengers," responded Mitchey, slightly indignantly.

"You said cruise-*type* ships. Meaning maybe you weren't so sure that what you saw really were cruise ships. What can you remember about them?"

She thought.

"I didn't see that many ships really. Just a few. I can fly pretty low and pretty slow in the Cub. I can circle things at less than 40 miles per hour if I'm careful not to make very steep turns.

"Whenever I saw these bigger ships, I'd circle them, you know, to give the passengers a thrill and all. Most of the ships had lots of passengers on deck, and they'd wave back." She paused a moment. "But there was one ship where only a few passengers were on deck waving. Seemed a little odd to me, because passengers generally like to look at the whales and the scenery, too. There are usually a lot of them on deck. But on that one ship there wasn't much activity on deck." She shrugged. "It seemed odd, but it did look like a cruise ship to me."

"Anything else?" asked Dad.

"Well, it seemed strange that it wasn't moving. You know, most cruise ships don't seem to sit at anchor. You can see their wakes as they move through the water. But maybe they were looking at something."

"Mitchey," asked my Dad, "Do you remember if that ship was in a cove or out in open water?"

"Come to think of it, that ship was anchored in a bay. And the bay was part of an island. But there were so many islands out there, that I'd be hard pressed to tell you which one island it was."

"Could you find its location again?"

"I'm not sure I could find its location. But I'm certain it was in the Prince William Sound area," she said, "It was near one of those big glaciers that falls into the ocean."

"Could it have been near the Malaspina Glacier?" asked Dad.

"I'm not sure I know which one is the Malaspina Glacier, there are so many of them," she said.

"Boy, if you were from Alaska, you'd know the Malaspina Glacier," I said. "It's bigger than Rhode Island and kind of hard to miss. I can find it on any map."

She laughed.

"I could probably find the location, again, but not on a map. I would have to fly out there and check out the area," she said.

"Unfortunately," said Dad, "the weather in that area is often poor. You got a lucky break having clear and sunny skies along the coast. We'll probably need the same sunny weather if we want to have a look."

"So what are you thinking?" asked Mitchey.

"Trying to figure out if this fits with some of the rumors I've been hearing about."

"What rumors?" I asked. I liked to hear all about the stuff Dad did at work. Mostly, it was better than TV.

"Well, son, rumors are just that. Often-times, you just can't believe them, and if you spread a rumor you are bound to hurt someone, even though you didn't mean to. Just the rumor can hurt folks. And rumors are often twisted so far that it's difficult to make sense of them," Dad said.

"But in police work, you have to listen to rumors, don't you?" I said.

"That's right, pal," responded Dad. "Bits and pieces of rumors can often lead us to find the answers to our questions. It's hard work separating the fact from the fiction."

"What have you heard?" asked Mitchey.

"Alaska is a very rich state in terms of natural resources," said Dad. "Nickel, gold, uranium, platinum, silver, trees, fish, probably even diamonds.

You name it, and most likely you'll find it in some commercial quantity in Alaska. Other countries would like to have access to those resources, and, with today's technology, they could pretty easily locate those minerals. But they couldn't buy or mine the restricted ones. Getting the exploration permits is difficult right now. But we've heard rumors that other countries may be doing some secret exploring anyway.

"Mitchey, did you happen to notice the name of that ship?" Dad asked.

"No, I didn't," she said. "I made just one pass over it and headed out to the northwest. No one seemed interested in me, so I wasn't really interested in them."

"Maybe it's just a coincidence, maybe not. Maybe someone was interested in you after all," mused Dad. "I'll check it out tomorrow. For now, we need to find someone to repair your plane."

4
The Town of Girdwood

Can't you do it?" I asked Dad.

"No, son, this plane's going to need new wiring to get back in the air. We'll have to get back to town and see if Roger Spernak will come out and do it. It's also getting late. You both must be hungry."

"I'm starved," I said.

Dad laughed and said, "That doesn't surprise me."

"It doesn't seem late," said Mitchey. "It's still pretty bright."

"The sun stays up until 11 p.m. this time of year in Alaska," I told her.

"Let's get the plane tied down," said Dad. Mitchey helped Dad push the Cub over to a sheltered area by the edge of the meadow and tied down the tail wheel and the wings.

"What about my stuff?" asked Mitchey.

"It'll be fine," said Dad. "Just don't leave any food in the plane. It might attract one of our wildlife friends. Bears are especially curious. If they smell food in there, they might treat it more like a sandwich than a flying machine."

I helped Mitchey haul her food box back to the Jeep.

As we headed down the road, Dad said to Mitchey, "I've seen some of that mountain country in Idaho. It's really rugged and beautiful. But the mountains there are every bit as unforgiving as they are here for pilots who misjudge the weather or their own abilities. You must do quite a bit of flying up there to have landed here like you did."

Mitchey nodded. "I fly sometimes for Mike's McCall Air Taxi, sometimes in a Super Cub. But I make deliveries in a Cessna 185," she said. The Cessna "Skywagon" is a big airplane. It seats four or five and holds loads of gear.

Dad was concentrating on a difficult stretch of road, and things got quiet for a while. When it got easier, Mitchey asked, "How far is it to town?"

"Not far, really," said Dad. "Just about 15 miles once we pass the old mine. We should be there in less than an hour."

"What town is it?" asked Mitchey.

"Girdwood," I told her.

Girdwood is about 50 miles southeast of Anchorage just off the only main road, Alaska Highway 1. It's an old mining town founded by early white settlers in the 1890s. The town sits at the base of a beautiful range of peaks in the Chugach Mountains. The ski area there, called Alyeska, has some of the finest ski terrain in North America—almost 3,000 vertical feet of skiing from the top to the bottom.

Girdwood has a population of about 800, but it's a hit with tourists in winter and summer. Skiers love the dry snow on top. Sightseers love the surrounding peaks that rise out of Cook Inlet and the huge, bluish-white, hanging glaciers that cascade off those alpine mountains.

"Dad says that the skiing's good in Idaho," I said. "Do you ski?"

"Mike Franklin and I used to ski together as kids. Actually, I was a much better cross-country skier," said Mitchey.

"We ski," I said looking over at Dad. "I can
ski any run on the mountain, and I can almost catch
Dad in the ski races."

Dad smiled but rolled his eyes at the same time.

"The kid is getting really good," he said,
glancing back at me. "Too good. He almost beat
me down the mountain last year." Dad smiled.
"Someday, he might even be as good as Tommy
Moe." Being compared to Tommy Moe, who won
gold and silver medals in the 1994 Olympics, *really*
made me feel good.

"Tommy's from around here, isn't he?" asked
Mitchey.

"He grew up in Girdwood," I told her. The TV
commentators always say he's from Palmer, Alaska.
But he's really from our town.

"Tommy is awesome! Mitchey, you should see
how fast he skis," I said. "He just flies down the
mountain. Dad used to race, too. He taught me to
ski when I was two."

Mitchey chuckled and asked, "You guys heard
the three most fearsome words in skiing?"

"Sure," Dad and I responded at the same time,
"*Follow me, Dad*!" And we all laughed together.

It was early evening when we pulled up to the
house. Dad had offered Mitchey our extra bedroom
for the night, and she had accepted.

"Boy, I'm glad we're home," I said. "I'm really hungry."

Dad laughed. "You're always hungry. I think you have a hollow leg."

"Mom used to say that it was just because I was a growing boy," I said. Mitchey looked puzzled. "My mom died a while back," I told her. "Now Dad and I sort of take care of each other."

"Who does the cooking?" asked Mitchey.

Dad laughed. "We live like bachelors, so that means we get lots of burgers for dinner."

Mitchey smiled and said, "Do you like burgers?"

"Yeah," I said, "but I like pizza more. And we get that pretty regularly, too." Bachelor life isn't all that tough, I thought.

Our house is a two-story, three-bedroom log cabin. Dad had bought it about ten years before, when it was just a little ski cabin. It's still kind of small, but Dad put on an addition when I was born. He says it will be his only expedition into house construction.

The living room is downstairs, along with the kitchen and the guest bedroom. Upstairs are Dad's bedroom and mine. We have a pretty good view of Cook Inlet from the upper balcony. We're close enough to the ski mountain that we can ski home when there is enough snow on the streets.

We hauled Mitchey's gear up to the house. Dad did most of the hauling. He's still pretty fit from working out four or five times a week. He says it not only makes him feel physically good, it helps him maintain a positive mental attitude.

I helped Mitchey stow her gear in the extra bedroom, while Dad called Roger Spernak, the mechanic and owner of the local air service. He worked on Dad's planes. Mr. Spernak had extra wiring for the magnetos and said he'd go out with us in the morning to fix up Mitchey's airplane.

We pulled up some fresh lettuce, cauliflower and radishes from the garden, and Dad made a great dinner of burgers and other good stuff.

"That was great," said Mitchey when we'd finished. "Didn't know how hungry I was."

"Are you too full to play some street hockey?" I asked.

"I'd love to," she said.

"I'll ref," said Dad.

Mitchey turned out to be pretty good for a girl. But I still beat her three goals to two. She could hardly get a shot past my deadly goaltending.

After the game, we went back in and I went off to bed. I left Dad and Mitchey talking in the living room.

Mitchey had been around hockey and skiing. She was okay by me.

5
Fixing the Cub

When I came downstairs early the next morning, Dad and Mitchey were already drinking coffee at the breakfast table. Mitchey looked up and said, "How about sourdough pancakes and eggs for breakfast?"

"Well, sure!" I said. "No self-respecting kid passes up pancakes and eggs—especially when someone else is doing the making." She laughed and got up to get things started.

Breakfast was a treat! When we finished eating, Dad called some friends in Valdez. I heard him ask questions about activity out at the airport two nights before.

"What did you find out?" I asked, when he finally hung up and came back to the table.

"Turns out that there were a couple of guys hanging out at the airport very late. In a small town like Valdez, people notice those things," he said to Mitchey. "They landed in a red amphibious plane." That's a plane that can land on land or water. Dad says that, in a pinch, they can even land on snow if they keep their wheels up.

"How can anyone remember that?" asked Mitchey.

"Small planes and strangers are not unusual during the summer months in Alaska," said Dad. "But these guys didn't fill up with gas or really even chat with anyone at the airport. Now gas is a pretty precious commodity in remote parts of Alaska. Pilots just about always fill their tanks, whether they need it or not. That's why the kid who pumps gas down there noticed. But he didn't give it all that much attention. He just figured they were heading into town for some reason or another."

The amphib left about two hours after it landed, said Dad, and no one seemed to know where it went, though he did talk to someone who recalled seeing an amphibious plane heading southeast along the shoreline late that night. Amphibians are unique-looking planes. I guess people don't forget when they see one.

After another cup of coffee, Dad got back on the phone and called the Federal Aeronautics Administration, called F.A.A. for short, to report the problem with Mitchey's plane.

"I don't want to make trouble for you," he told Mitchey, "but I'm pretty sure your plane was tampered with. I have to report it to the F.A.A."

He was immediately patched through to Kelly Ringer, the F.A.A. duty officer, and told her what had happened. Kelly told him to take pictures of the engine before the repair was made. Then she promised Dad she'd do some checking with folks in Anchorage and Valdez to see if she could learn more about the red amphibian or possible activity off the coast.

As soon as we finished breakfast, we headed back out to the plane. The weather was a little bit overcast, but we didn't need to put the top up on the jeep. Mr. Spernak and I were in the back. He didn't like the ride much. He grunted the whole way, especially during the last part of the ride, which was very bumpy.

"If it wasn't for the challenge of fixing a plane stranded in some far-out mountain valley," he said, "I wouldn't have come."

When we finally got to the clearing, Mr. Spernak shook his head. "You were sure lucky, little lady, to pull off a dead stick landing out here. I seen many pilots just plow it in. Well, at least I seen the results of their flying skills." He laughed.

Dad helped Mr. Spernak remove the cowling. After they laid it on the grass, Dad photographed the engine and the burned-through wiring.

"Done a pretty good job on that wiring," said Mr. Spernak. "I wouldn't have figured it out in a crash. But it was a sloppy job, if they meant to really try to kill the pilot. Anyone who knows planes knows this plane can land in tough, rough spots. They must have been in a hurry."

"I'm glad they were," said Mitchey.

"Roger," said Dad, "Let's keep this to ourselves. I'm not sure what happened here, or why, but the fewer people who know about it, and know about Mitchey surviving the crash, the better." Mr. Spernak nodded and set about repairing the damage.

The repair took only about an hour. Mr. Spernak explained his work to me as he went. Just like Dad, he asked me for this tool and that, and I would try to find the right ones in his tool box.

Once I thought I heard a model plane, the kind

that are radio controlled. I looked around to say something to Dad and discovered that he and Mitchey were sitting in the Jeep talking. They certainly were laughing a lot.

"I wouldn't trade this job for anything," said Mr. Spernak. I turned back to him.

"How'd you learn?" I asked.

"Learned aviation mechanics in the military. Then got the rest of my training at the community college in Anchorage. Job lets me live just about anywhere I want, and earn a decent living, too. And I get to meet all kinds of neat people. A kind of bonus," he said.

When Mr. Spernak was finished, we walked to the Jeep.

"She's all right now," he said.

"Mitchey, why don't I fly the plane back to Girdwood," said Dad.

"Thanks, but I'll be fine."

Dad didn't argue, but he went out and paced off the take-off area for the little Cub, about 600 feet on this terrain. He marked it with a stick, and then walked off another 400 feet for safety.

"You'll need to make a sharp left turn while you're still below the tree line," he told her. "Then fly down river. It may be tricky at slow speed."

"I haven't done this a zillion times," she said, "but it's not too complicated as long as I don't lose power."

"You won't lose no power," said Mr. Spernak. "I'll make sure everything is tops before you make your run up."

"Okay," Dad said. "The approach into the Girdwood strip can be tricky, too, because of the power lines and the old court house that sit right at the end of the air strip. It's great for Cubs, but if you come in too hot and fast, and you don't drop her down quick after the courthouse, well, it won't be a pretty sight, what with the mud hole they call a pond at the other end of the runway."

"I'll watch it," said Mitchey, as she climbed into the plane and buckled up her seat belt. She took a few minutes to check things over and then cranked the engine. The cowl was still open, and Mr. Spernak checked out the engine with her help. After about five minutes, Mr. Spernak told her to shut it down.

"Anything wrong?" Mitchey asked.

"Nope," said Mr. Spernak. "Just didn't want to try to shut the cowling with that prop spinning out there. You never know about these things. Best to shut her down first."

Mitchey nodded, and Mr. Spernak buttoned up the engine.

A few moments later, Mitchey was taxiing a short distance to the edge of the meadow. She was doing her run up and engine check along the way.

"That's a good sign," said Dad to me. "Mark of a pilot who cares about her prop. Remember, partner, run ups are always important because they are a part of the preflight check of the engine, prop, and the instruments. Problem is, run-ups are tough on props when you do them on turf or gravel. The prop can actually suck up a rock or some other object, and it's easy for the prop to get nicked or damaged. When you are on a rough surface like this field, it's best to do your run-up while the plane is rolling. But that takes lots of practice, too, because you have to concentrate on what you are doing *and* where you are headed."

Mitchey looked down the field toward the river. I could see the concentration on her face, even at this distance. She poured on the throttle, and the little plane accelerated toward us. And, by gosh, she lifted off right where Dad had placed the stick!

Slowly she climbed toward the creek and the opposite hillside. As she gained speed, she turned left out over the river and disappeared behind the tall trees. A moment later we saw her climbing above the trees. She made a pass back toward us at about 500 feet, heading south for Girdwood.

Mr. Spernak, Dad, and I piled back in the Jeep, and headed back to town. Dad was quiet for a while. Then he said to me, "Her registration numbers were really visible from the ground, weren't they?" Older planes have their registration numbers painted on the underside of the wings. Each letter is about two feet high.

I thought I knew what Dad was getting at. Someone had seen Mitchey's plane, written down the numbers, and then somehow had found it and tampered with the engine. Dad thought she had seen something, even though she didn't quite know what she'd seen. My thought was that someone didn't want her to tell what they thought she knew.

6

Kidnapped in Girdwood

The Girdwood air strip runs practically right down the center of town. In the 1920s, when the U.S. mail was just starting to use airplanes, the postal service decided that Girdwood was a good refueling stop for their planes heading north and south along the Alaska Railroad line. For navigation, the pilots followed the railroad tracks. It was really important to have tracks in sight during bad visibility, like snow or fog. Dad says the pilots could even land on the railroad tracks in an emergency. But it was dangerous and tricky because of the ties and the rails.

The hangars at the air strip were built by the postal service to protect the planes from snow and ice at night. Dad's office now owns one of them, and he keeps both planes, the Cessna 185 and the Piper Super Cub, inside.

Dad keeps the 185 on skis in the winter, and on wheels in the summer. It has dual controls— two steering wheels that come out of the dash— and two sets of rudder pedals with brakes.

The Super Cub is Dad's pride and joy. It carries two people in tandem, the passenger up front and the pilot in the back. The Cub is flown with a stick that comes up between your knees, not a control wheel. Although the pilot flies the Cub from the back, there is a stick up front, too, and a full set of controls. When Dad and I are flying the Cub, he lets me take the stick.

Mitchey had already found a place to tie down her plane by the time we arrived at the air strip. Dad dropped Mr. Spernak off by the hangar, then drove over to pick up Mitchey at her Cub.

"Roger is going to come over later and have another look at your plane, just to make sure everything is operating fine," Dad said to Mitchey as she got into the Jeep. "I'm going to drive into Anchorage to do some checking with the F.A.A.

and the Coast Guard. Why don't you have Andy give you a tour of Girdwood and the ski area?"

"It's still early in the day, so that would be super!" Mitchey exclaimed.

"The ski resort's really grown in recent years," Dad told Mitchey. "You wouldn't recognize it from the way it looked 20 years ago. Last year, the resort's new owners built an aerial tramway. Now that they have completed their resort hotel, the area is attracting tourists from all over the world."

"That should be good for the town," said Mitchey.

"I don't know," said Dad. "I've got mixed feelings about tourism."

"Why's that?"

"I think the increased activity is good," he said, "But not the low-paying jobs. It's tough to keep Girdwood a family community what with the jobs paying only minimum wage up at the ski area. And the resort's the biggest employer in the valley, so they really will have an impact."

"Yes, I can understand that," said Mitchey.

"We've got a couple of mountain bikes back at the house," I said. "Let's cruise town and then ride up to the ski area on the bikes."

"Well, like when do we get started?" asked Mitchey.

"Well, like right now!" I said.

Dad laughed and said, "I'll take you two back to the house, then I'll head to Anchorage."

As we drove, Mitchey asked Dad, "What are you looking for in town?"

"Just following a hunch, really," Dad said. "If that ship isn't really a cruise ship, maybe the Coast Guard has been keeping track of its position on radar. If so, I'd like to see the radar track on it and find out what the Coast Guard thinks the vessel is doing.

"I work with different people in the customs service, the national fisheries folks, and the FBI, on occasion. I'll check with those folks, too."

"Do you think that boat was fishing illegally, like maybe stealing salmon or something?" I asked.

"Well, pal, I don't think they'd go to the trouble of using such a big ship if they were just poaching a few salmon," Dad said. "No, it would have to be something else. But, hey, we're not even sure that ship has anything to do with Mitchey's problem anyway."

Ten minutes after Dad dropped us off at the house, Mitchey and I were clipped into mountain bikes and were pedaling down the road to town. I showed her the general store, which has the best ice-cream cones in the world. Of course, we stopped to sample them.

We rode down past the little arts and crafts shops and stopped to look in the windows of several gift stores. I introduced Mitchey to some of my friends hanging out behind the World Cup Sports Shop on the basketball courts.

We toured past the old courthouse building, and stopped at the pioneer museum. Not only did it have displays from Girdwood's heyday as a mining town, but it also exhibits photos of some of the famous people who have grown up or lived in the Girdwood area. Finally we pedaled on up the road to Mt. Alyeska ski area.

During the summer, you can take bikes up on the tram, and ride down the ski runs. Mitchey said, "I've never ridden down a ski run, but I've seen the mountain bike racers on television."

"Yeah!" I said. "I've seen the Kamikaze downhill mountain bike race at Mammoth, California on TV. At Mammoth, the riders hit 55 miles an hour in some sections of the race course. But I'll bet our downhill runs are steeper and faster than theirs!"

Mitchey just rolled her eyes. "Go easy on me, okay?" she asked.

I laughed. "No problem," I said.

We got two one-way tickets for the tram,
grabbed our bikes and wheeled them up the ramp
to the tramway building. After we boarded, the
attendant closed the doors. Slowly, the tram glided
out from the building and began its ascent to the
summit of the ski area.

The vertical rise is almost a mile, and the
valley looks entirely different from way up in the
air than from on the ground.

The fifteen-mile long Winner Creek valley
starts at sea level at the Cook Inlet fjord of the
Turnagain Arm. The peaks, which rise dramati-
cally everywhere you look, are forested up to
about 1,500 feet. After that, it's Arctic tundra. The
valley is surrounded by glaciers. I pointed eight
of them out to Mitchey.

I've seen the view from the tram lots of times.
I'm kind of used to it. But going up with someone
who hasn't taken the ride before is a neat experience. They are really impressed. Mitchey was no
exception. About all she could say was, "Wow!"
"Oh, how beautiful!" "That is really spectacular."
"Wow, look at that!"

While Mitchey was exclaiming over the
scenery, I noticed a couple of guys on the tram
who looked like tourists. But they didn't seem to

be much interested in the view. The men were carrying small backpacks and cameras, but I didn't see either of them take a picture. They spent a lot of time whispering to each other, not like tourists at all. Some people are hard to impress, I thought.

The tram docked at the top terminal.

"I'm kind of hungry," I told Mitchey. "Want to get something to eat?"

"Sure," she said. "Lead the way."

We headed over to the old Round House restaurant at the top of the ski lifts. Mitchey and I ordered a couple of sandwiches and sodas, and then we took them outside on the deck to eat in the midday sun.

"So what's it like growing up in Alaska?" asked Mitchey as we ate.

"Girdwood's great," I told her. "The people are really neat, and there's lots of things to do. In the winter there's skiing and hockey. Then in the summer, I play street hockey with my friends. Or we ride our bikes down and go swimming in the gravel ponds along the main road. Because the sun's out so long in the summer, its natural warmth heats the water until it's almost bathtub temperature.

"Some people are pretty adventurous. They go wind-surfing out on Cook Inlet. Some of the boarders say it's almost as good as the wind-surfing down at the Columbia Gorge in Oregon. The winds sometimes blow 50 to 60 miles an hour. I really like to watch the board surfers jump waves and do flips in the heavy swells."

"The water must be cold," said Mitchey.

"It's so cold you could die in an instant if you weren't all bundled up in dry suits. But no one's ever been hurt at it. So folks feel it's pretty safe."

"What about school?" asked Mitchey.

"It's okay. I do pretty well at math. And I really like drawing pictures of houses. Dad said my great grandfather was a famous architect, so maybe that's what I'll grow up to be."

"I kind of got the feeling you'd like to be a pilot," said Mitchey.

"Well, that'd be pretty cool, too," I said. "I already know how to take off and fly both the Cub and the 185. Haven't quite got the landing down yet. I've followed Dad through lots of them, but I still can't control the rudders and the stick just right.

" 'Once you start your landing flare,' he says, 'keep that stick back. Don't release the pressure. Keep holding it back.' " Mitchey laughed as I imitated my dad's deep voice.

"Dad says it just takes practice. But it's tough to keep the nose and the wings straight. Especially because I still can't see over the nose of the plane during a three-point landing. Dad says that flying from the back seat, he can't see over the nose, either. He says you just have to get used to it. I'm not there, yet, but I'm not giving up!" I told her.

"You'll get it, I'm sure," said Mitchey.

"Someday, Dad says he'll have Mr. Spernak give me flying lessons. And I've written to the E.A.A., the F.A.A., and the Aircraft Owners and Pilots Association about scholarships. I figure maybe I can help push Dad's plans along."

"Was your dad raised in Alaska, too?" Mitchey asked.

"No, his folks moved up here when he was young. This is where he learned to ski. He was part of the national ski team. When he got older, his parents moved back down to the lower 48 states. But after college, Dad came back to Alaska. He said that sooner or later, the beauty of this valley would cause Girdwood to grow. And he wanted to be here to help out. He said he wanted to help protect it."

"You're pretty happy here then," she said.

"Yeah, mostly I am, I guess," I told her. "But sometimes I wish Mom was still here." Mitchey nodded.

While we talked, I noticed the two men from the tram sitting a distance away. Again I thought they were acting strangely. They didn't wander around the deck to look at the scenery or walk down into the mountain tundra, like most tourists.

"You ready for some downhill?" I asked Mitchey as we finished our lunch.

"Let's go," she said.

We put on our helmets, grabbed our bikes, and took off down the ski runs.

What a ride! We hauled buns. Mitchey caught on pretty fast.

"I like this!" she shouted to me. I could see that.

We leaped jumps and zoomed through water crossings. I kind of sneaked Mitchey into a cool, single-track route called the elevator. The track twists and turns through the underbrush and then drops really steeply through a rock outcropping. I made it okay, but Mitchey lost control on the last pitch and her bike slid out from underneath her. She slid the last ten feet, but she wasn't hurt. She laughed and I did, too, remembering my first time down the elevator.

That was the high point of the ride, and we started working our way back to the house to clean up. As we were going down one of the subdivision roads. Mitchey called to me, "Andy, there's a car right behind me. I think he's trying to get by."

We pulled over and stopped to let it pass. The car stopped, too, and two men started to get out. I recognized the men from the tram.

I began to get a really bad feeling. Then I saw that one of the men had a gun.

"Go, Mitchey! Run! One of them has a gun!" I yelled, and I took off on my bike. Mitchey jumped back on her bike and started off after me.

Having grown up in Girdwood, I knew the local streets like the back of my hand. Furiously, I pedaled to escape.

"Follow me, Mitchey!" I hollered. And she stuck right on my tail. Houses in Girdwood are far apart. The streets are dirt, and there are lots of forested areas between the homes.

The men jumped back in their car and took off after us. I cut up driveways and through back lots trying to lose them. Mitchey stayed right with me. But the men had a four-wheel drive, and they kept coming.

We were getting tired and I was getting desperate. As we raced across a road and into an alley, I ducked a tree branch but Mitchey didn't see it. It knocked her off her bike.

I screeched to a stop and yelled to her, but before I could do anything, the car stopped and the men jumped out. Mitchey had her bike back up, but they grabbed her before she could take off. They were pushing her into the back seat of their car.

"Get away from me! Let me go!" she yelled at the men.

"Run, Andy," she screamed as they shoved her into the back seat of their car.

But I couldn't let them just grab her. So I started back towards them on my bike. I managed to run into the driver just as he was getting into the car. My handlebar banged on his door, and the force of the impact knocked me over.

"Darn stupid kid," the man said as he started to reach for me. "I'll take care of your butt." I managed to scramble clear of his grip and saw that my bike was still intact. I jumped on it and headed back up the street, desperately trying to get away.

The driver slammed the car into reverse and accelerated the car backwards up the street toward me. I saw a big earthen berm off to one side and launched my bike over the top. The kidnappers couldn't follow me over that high spot, and I managed to escape behind several houses.

I could see them driving around looking for me. After a few minutes, they apparently gave up because I could see them through the trees driving off down the main highway.

7
Air Search

I jumped back on my bike and raced off toward the main road, but there was no way I was going to catch the escaping car.

The only chance I had to help Mitchey was to get to a radio or a telephone and somehow get help. I've got to get to Dad, I thought.

Girdwood houses are not really very close together. What we call a subdivision is really a sparse collection of cabins in the woods. So houses are kind of far apart, but you can usually see from one house to another through the trees and underbrush.

I skidded my bike into a turn and raced into
the yard of the nearest house. I banged on the door.
No one was home. Shoot! I said to myself. It could
take too much time to find someone home. So I
hopped back on my bike and rode to the next house
as fast as I could. No one home there, either. Our
house was only a block or so away, and Dad had a
radio and telephone in the downstairs study. So I
blasted off to our house.

I jumped off my bike in the dirt driveway and
it crashed to the ground behind me. I ran into the
house and called the marshal's office.

"I'm not sure where he is, Andy," said the
deputy on duty. "What's wrong? You sound upset."

I was almost out of breath, and my heart was
pounding, but in as calm a voice as I could, I explained
what had happened.

"Can you describe the car?"

"It was a black, four-wheel drive, I think," I
said.

"Did you get the license plate number?"

"Things were happening real fast, and I didn't
have time to look," I told him.

"What did the men look like?"

"I only saw the two of them on the mountain.
One was big and had on a red, lumberjack-type of

shirt. The other one was thin, about five foot eight. That guy was wearing a baseball hat. A blue one, I think. There was another man in the back seat of the car, but I couldn't make out any features. He reached out for Mitchey when the big guy pushed her into the car. I might have hurt the guy with the baseball cap when I hit the door. I tried to run him over with my bike."

"Where are you, Andy? Are you home?" he asked when I was done.

"Yeah."

"Is anyone with you?"

"No. Just me."

"Stay put. I'm sending someone out to be with you. He'll stay there until we can raise your dad. Until the deputy gets there, lock the doors."

In about ten minutes, the deputy came. Dad rushed in not long after. I guess he was on his way home, but had been out of radio distance because the big mountains along the highway from Anchorage tend to block radio signals.

"Are you okay?" he asked as he came through the door.

"I'm okay," I said. "But, Dad, they got Mitchey. They followed us up the mountain, then chased us through the subdivision. One of them had a gun.

"We tried to get away from them on our bikes, and we almost did, too, except that Mitchey ate it going around a corner. I think she hit a low tree branch and got knocked off her bike.

"I was really scared, Dad. I tried to get the license plate number," I told him.

"You did great, pal. These guys sure act like pros. I'm really proud of you. I wonder how they found Mitchey. How could they have known where she landed the plane?"

Dad was shaking, and I knew he was angry. I'd seen it before. But he quickly gained his composure. He sat down by me at the kitchen table.

"I want you to know something, Bud," he said. "I am really upset that these people have kidnapped Mitchey. I like her a lot. And it's not your fault, either. You did the best you could.

"But I'm really ticked they would go after my boy. I love you more than anything," he said.

I really felt better that I wasn't to blame. And it always made me feel good to hear my dad say how much he loved me.

"Well, this just proves Mitchey must have seen something that scared them. Why else would they be coming after her like this?" I said.

"I think you're right on, pal. Whoever took

Mitchey probably wants to find out what she knows and what she has told," he said. "They may come after us next. More likely, though, they'll pull up stakes and hightail it out of here. Either way, it doesn't look good for Mitchey."

I didn't like the sound of that.

"Let's just make like Chuck Norris—or Rambo—or someone, and go in there and get her out!" I said.

Dad smiled a little at that comment.

"I'd like nothing better, pal, but we really don't know that Mitchey has been taken to some ship out in the Sound. We need some proof, a lead of some kind," Dad said.

Just then the phone rang, and Dad took the call.

"The State Troopers found the car," he said to me. "It was stolen earlier today. They dumped it in a pond near the highway. That pond's big enough for an amphibious plane to land and take off."

"Deputy," he said, "See if you can dig up any witnesses who might have seen a plane like we talked about flying along the Arm today."

As soon as he hung up, Dad called the Coast Guard and asked them to be on the alert for suspicious activity around ships out of Valdez.

"What did they say?" I asked.

"Their nearest cutter is probably 18 hours away. They said it would probably be futile to send the ship in, considering the size of the area and the time it would take to get there," he said.

"But they have to help," I said.

"The Coast Guard is stretched pretty thin, pal. Remember it's commercial fishing season. They don't have many ships out here. But they are going to try. They'll let us know."

I was getting really frustrated when the phone rang again. It was Dad's friend, Kelly Ringer, from the F.A.A.

Dad made a lot of "Uh huh" sounds, then, "You're sure about that? Okay, Kelly, thanks. I owe you one." He hung up.

"What's up?" I asked.

"Kelly went back and reviewed some of the F.A.A. radar tapes. Turns out that in certain areas they can get some radar coverage to the surface of the water within 10 miles of the coast. Kelly noticed that several nights ago, there was a very faint radar track of a light plane coming into Valdez from somewhere out in the sound. The time is about the same as when the gas jockey in Valdez reported seeing an amphibious plan at the airport. They have a track both coming and going, so we have the general bearing the plane was flying."

"Let's go!" I said jumping up. "What are we waiting for? They've got Mitchey. Now we know where she is!"

"I'm as anxious as you are, pal," Dad said to me. "But that was several nights ago. They may have moved their whole operation by now. That's a pretty big area, and searching it won't be easy."

"But Dad, you said yourself that they'll probably get rid of her!"

"If I were them," he said, "I'd hold her hostage just in case I needed a bargaining chip. But I think I have an idea. Grab your coat and let's go."

"Where to?" I asked as I followed him out the door.

"Out to Elmendorf Air Force Base in Anchorage."

Instead of our Jeep, we climbed in his patrol car and sped off.

As we drove I asked Dad, "Did you learn anything from either the Coast Guard or the F.A.A. while you were in town?"

"Not much, really," he said. "The Coast Guard had nothing unusual on their radar tapes. Ships come and go. Some linger for a day or two just looking at the sights in Prince William Sound. A ship disguised as a cruise ship could slip into U.S. waters for a day or two, support a research effort, and then leave without much notice.

"There isn't much radar coverage at lower altitudes out there because of all the mountains and inlets. That's why the F.A.A. didn't think there'd be much on their tapes. I'm glad Kelly found those tracks.

"Both the F.A.A. and the Coast Guard are concerned about this," Dad said. "Partly because of the tampering with Mitchey's airplane, but more importantly, because they've heard reports that foreign countries are trying to get precious minerals from the United States for their own research purposes. They think it's entirely possible that a ship outfitted to look like a cruise ship could be supporting some kind of secret underwater research effort. They're starting to work with other federal agencies on this investigation. But it will probably take them a long time to get a handle on it."

"Why don't they just go out there and search the ship?" I asked.

"Without some kind of proof, no one can board a ship in U.S. waters and just search it," Dad said. "Most cruise ships travel between Alaska and Vancouver, British Columbia. Once they leave U.S. waters and go out beyond the 13-mile limit, the U.S. loses all jurisdiction, too."

"Then there's nothing we can do?"

"I didn't say that. That's why we're going to Elmendorf."

Once we cleared the other side of town and had a line of sight towards Anchorage, Dad placed a call on his radio phone.

"Colonel Frank Doctor, please," he said into the telephone. "Yes, please tell him this is Marshal Armstrong. Sam Armstrong. Thanks. Yes, I'll wait."

"Who's Colonel Doctor?" I asked.

"An old friend of mine in Air Force Intelligence," he said.

"Hi, Witch," he said switching to the phone.

Witch? I thought.

"Yeah. Actually, no. Things aren't going too good," said Dad. "Look, I need your help. I can't really explain it all over this phone, but I'd like to hitch a ride on one of your recon missions. Yeah, that's right, it is really urgent. Great. We'll be there in less than an hour. Yeah, I've got Andy with me. You think maybe we can put him to work? Great. See you soon."

"Okay, Andy, let's hit it," Dad said. He hit the lights and the siren, and we began a rocket ride down the highway to Anchorage.

8

Virtual Reality

Why do you call Colonel Doctor, 'Witch'?"
I asked.

"Witch is the nickname his Air Force buddies
gave him during his flight training, partly because
of his last name," Dad explained. "But Colonel
Doctor is one of the top back-seaters in the Air Force.
In the back seat of a fighter, he runs the radios and
radar. He's also the weapons systems officer. They
named him Witch partly because of the magic he
works in the back seat."

"So why'd you call him?" I asked.

"Witch is one of the top reconnaissance officers in the U.S. He operates Air Force air intelligence over all of the North Pacific, the Bering Sea, and the Arctic Ocean. Even though what used to be the Soviet Union is not a threat any more, Witch still maintains a high level of intelligence gathering for our country. If we are being 'invaded,' even by a single ship at sea, Witch will do what he can to help us."

"How?" I asked.

"Well, since the land-based radar doesn't get us the coverage we need, I figure the fastest way to cover that area is to get out there in a fast jet and do a visual inspection. Take some pictures. Also, with a jet, we might be able to scare up some kind of reaction from the people on the ship to confirm our suspicions."

About then we arrived at the entrance gate to Elmendorf. Dad showed his marshal's badge to the gate guard. Then we followed a pilot car to a large, gray building alongside the air base's two-mile-long runway.

Colonel Doctor met us at a side door of the building. He greeted Dad with a strong handshake and a big bear hug.

"Cowboy," he said, "how you doing, buddy?"

Dad seemed a little embarrassed by being called Cowboy.

"You must be Andy," he said to me, shaking my hand as he led us down a hall to the ready room.

"You still current on your ejection seat training, Cowboy?" asked the Witch.

"You've got the records, Witch. I'm pretty sure I got a checkout within the last six months," said Dad.

There was somebody waiting for us in the ready room.

"Cowboy, this is Captain Snake Bonner. Snake, this is Sam Armstrong—Marshal Armstrong from down Girdwood way—and his son Andy." Captain Bonner shook hands just as another pilot walked into the room.

"And this is Captain Allen Murdoch, call sign Mudhole." Dad shook hands with Captain Murdoch. "Murdoch is our top single-seater. He's taken top honors twice at Red Flag. Mudhole is a graduate of the Air Force's Fighter Weapons School; and he is working with us to test several of our experimental aircraft.

"Okay, Armstrong, now tell us what this is all about."

So Dad gave the pilots and Colonel Doctor a

brief review of what had been happening and told them why we had come.

"Can't hurt to take a look," said the colonel. "Bonner will be your driver and Mudhole will fly your wing, just to keep you clean and safe. There are no better sled drivers than these two," said the colonel.

"Suit up, Cowboy," said Mudhole.

Dad stripped down to his underwear and reached for the military-issue flight suit that was waiting for him. He seemed to know exactly how to put on the G-suit over his flight suit.

"You've done this before," said Captain Bonner.

"I've had a few rides in fighters," said Dad. "Once thought about going into the Air Force to become a fighter pilot. But when it came to a choice between going into the service or skiing, I chose racing." The three fliers laughed.

What Dad didn't say, but that I knew, was that he didn't regret his decision. When it came right down to it, he said, he probably couldn't have brought himself to kill people in war.

The colonel clapped me on the shoulder.

"Your dad is a natural pilot," he said. "When he's flying, he just wears the airplane. It becomes a part of him, like an extension of his body." Dad seemed embarrassed, but the colonel didn't seem to notice. "Great pilots don't control their planes, and the planes don't control great pilots," he told me. "Great pilots feel everything through the plane, like the airplane is a sixth sense, or an extension of the mind and the spirit."

I knew what Colonel Doctor was talking about. I've seen Dad sense things when we fly.

"Yep," said Colonel Doctor, "Your dad is one of the most gifted pilots I've ever met."

As Dad was getting his G-suit adjusted, he turned to Captain Murdoch and asked, "So Murdoch, how'd you get the call sign 'Mudhole'?"

Murdoch said a bit sheepishly, "Has to do with an interesting adventure I had during my flight training. Let's just say we got a little stuck in an out-of-the-way place." Murdoch smiled a big, toothy grin.

Dad said, "I think I get the picture," just as he finished suiting up.

"Snake, how long before you're airborne?" asked the colonel.

"Probably 60 minutes," said the Snake. "Thirty minutes to get the brief. Twenty to do the preflight, ten minutes to get the fires lit, taxi, and takeoff."

"Right," said the colonel, looking at his watch. "Andy, let's move out."

"Aren't you going along, too?" I asked the colonel.

"Andy, you and I are going to monitor the flight from our new control area," he said.

Well, that certainly intrigued me.

"Good luck, Dad," I called as the colonel and I headed out of the ready room.

We went down a hall, turned left, and stopped in front of a door marked *Secure Area. Authorized Personnel Only.* Colonel Doctor entered a code on a keypunch pad on the wall and then put his hand up to a screen that was also on the wall. "Frank Doctor, Colonel, U.S. Air Force," he said into a small speaker mounted on the wall next to screen. The door unlocked. He turned the handle, and we entered a large room with a couple of big, boxy objects in the middle. Both boxes were raised up on stilts and surrounded by platforms where technicians probably could stand.

"Are those simulators?" I asked.

"In a manner of speaking. They're very advanced. We can program them as full-motion, full-video simulators for pilot training. But these two machines are actually remote cockpits from which we can pilot—from a location such as this room— several of our specially-outfitted F-15 Strike Eagle fighter jets without putting a live pilot in the cockpit.

"Over there, by the wall, is the super computer that runs these cockpits. It's hooked into a sophisticated communication and control mechanism. The sensors and computers on the Eagles allow us to fly along with the mission and observe everything they see. Or we can pilot them as drones, without pilots."

This is really cool, I thought.

"Through the simulator/cockpit dynamics, it feels like we are actually on board the fighter jet. But the most important feature," explained the colonel, "is that all of this is linked to a set of two helmets which we wear in those cockpits right here in this room.

"These are 'virtual reality' helmets. That means that the environment in which we are going to sit will be nearly identical to the one your dad will be in.

"This is cutting-edge technology, Andy. We're going for an actual 'flight.'"

"You mean 'we' meaning you and me? I'm going to fly an F-15?" I asked incredulously.

"Yes, I mean you and I. It is important that you go along on this flight because you may see something that our boys in the air won't because they will be busy concentrating on their flying," said the colonel.

I was totally blown away. Playing nintendo on the TV would never seem the same.

"While we're in the cockpit/simulator and wearing our special helmets, we can have the computer stop on the visual, enhance it, zoom in, whatever we want it to do," said the colonel. "So let's get set up."

Just then another person walked up.

"Andy, this is Joan Kraft. She is a civilian contractor from McDonnell Douglas. Joan, this is Andy Armstrong. Andy is going to help us on this recon mission."

"Mr. Armstrong, it's good to have you here in our facility," said Ms. Kraft. She called me "Mister," I thought. That was too cool. But I tried not to show it.

"Let's step over here to the cockpit door, and I'll explain a few things about what is about to happen," said Ms. Kraft.

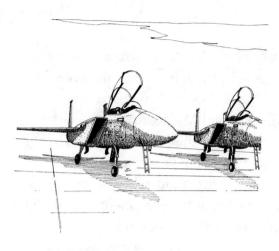

9

In the Cockpit

The earliest virtual reality systems," said Joan Kraft, "were linked to our cockpit simulators, but the images were very crude compared to what you're going to experience. That's because the images you will see in this simulator will be almost three dimensional. The early computer images used colored stick visuals.

"The programs we use today are linked to video cameras on board the aircraft. What you see in the simulator is actually what you would see if you were in the aircraft. Linking the flight systems to the virtual reality cockpit and the computer gives us far more flexibility with our aircraft and with the pilot."

"Colonel Doctor said that using this system you can fly the airplane without the pilot," I said.

"Yes, and we have tested that now a number of times," said Ms. Kraft.

"Does that mean the planes can fight in a battle, too, without a pilot?" I asked.

Ms. Kraft nodded. "The helmet supports a number of control mechanisms for both recon and aggressor modes," she said.

"When you say 'aggressor mode,' you mean when the pilot is attacking another aircraft?" I asked.

"It's a bit more than that, Andy. The system can be programmed for the aggressor mode any time the pilot is in a hostile environment and might have to take evasive action, defend himself, or defend others," responded Ms. Kraft. "Of course, recon is often done in a hostile environment.

"Problem is, even though this system is just like being there, being there for real is still the most important element in any successful mission," said Ms. Kraft. "All the super computers in the world are still no match for the decision-making process of the human brain and the human senses. We need those human feelings to help us make the right decisions. We get the best of both worlds when we combine our system here with the pilot in the aircraft."

"Kind of like double-trouble," I said.

All the technicians in the room laughed at that. Ms. Kraft went on to explain to me the basic functions of the controls in the simulator. There were so many switches, I couldn't really keep up with what she was saying. But some of the controls looked familiar.

"Ms. Kraft," I said, "I've got the game called "F-15 Strike Eagle" on my computer at home. The basic gauges here look the same, including the heads-up display and the navigation equipment. But this is a whole bunch more complicated."

"I've played that game," she said. "It really does come close to simulating flight in the F-15. I think you can learn great stuff from computer programs which simulate the aviation environment. In a way, these simulators are just very expensive computer games. But because this cockpit/simulator is linked to the actual airplane, it is not a game. It's the real thing," said Ms. Kraft.

"Your dad's a pilot, isn't he?" she asked. "Have you done much flying with him?"

"You bet," I said. "I can fly both our Super Cub and the Cessna 185."

"Great," said Ms. Kraft, pointing to the control stick in the cockpit area. "Since you've flown a Cub, you know how to use a stick like the one in this simulator."

I nodded.

"OK, then," she said, "let's get this helmet on, and I'll explain its use."

Ms. Kraft lifted the helmet off the cart that was on the platform next to the simulator. It was like something out of the movie *Star Wars*, kind of a Darth Vader-type helmet with several big cables coming out of the sides. The front had a see-through visor—really quite large—that gave good visibility to the front, up and down, and to the sides.

"Okay, Andy, I'm going to place this on your head. Good. Now let's make sure it is snug under your chin. Feel okay?" she asked.

"It feels pretty good!" I said, hearing my own muffled voice.

"We are not going to use the kind of oxygen mask that fits over your nose and mouth, the ones the pilots up there will be wearing. Inside their masks are voice-activated mikes. Since you won't be wearing the mask, I'm going to attach this mike around your neck."

"Will I be able to talk to the pilots?"

Ms. Kraft said, "Absolutely."

"Now I'm going to power up the helmet." Ms. Kraft motioned to a technician standing near a computer display, and the helmet lit up inside. There were several different displays inside the visor, mainly along the sides and the top.

"In a moment, your heads-up display will appear on the inside of the visor," said Ms. Kraft. "Our old heads-up display was projected on the front of the airplane's canopy or on a small screen in front of the pilot. However, when the pilot turned his head, he lost touch with vital information such as air speed, weapons stores, and location of the enemy. By projecting this information inside the helmet, no matter where the pilot looks, he has the supporting information to help him make quick, possibly lifesaving decisions.

"Alex," she said to a technician, "bring up a bogey in the simulator, say at Andy's six o'clock. Bogey is air force lingo for an enemy object like an airplane or a missile.

A small red light appeared at the bottom of my visor. I could just see it if I looked straight ahead.

"Do you see the red light, Andy?" Ms. Kraft asked.

I nodded.

"Andy, you need to speak clearly," she said. "We can't see you nod in the simulator."

"Yes, I see the light," I responded.

"If you look straight at the light you can see it clearly. But when you look straight ahead, you'll be able to just sense the light in your peripheral vision," Ms. Kraft explained. "Now swivel your head," she directed.

As I moved my head to the left, the light moved around the visor to the left.

"In this mode," said Ms. Kraft," when the pilot turns his or her head to look for the bogey, the light moves around the helmet. The pilot knows that when the light is on the top of his visor he should be looking straight at the bogey. Some pilots prefer that the light doesn't move when they look away from the front of the plane. That way they always know where the bogey or bandit is relative to the front of their aircraft. We give them that option, and several others."

"Way cool," I said.

Ms. Kraft chuckled.

"Okay, let's have you climb into the simulator and seat yourself. Careful with your feet. Good. Now let's adjust your controls."

In a modern jet fighter, the seat does not move fore and aft, rudder controls move closer and farther away from the pilot. Ms. Kraft adjusted the controls for me until they felt comfortable. I was surprised they fit my five-foot three-inch kid's body and said so.

"Many of our top fighter pilots are relatively small. Shorter bodies seem to handle the stress of high G-forces really well. So aircraft are manufactured to fit a wide range of body heights, especially the smaller ones like yours." She chuckled.

"Okay, now, let me strap you in. You'll feel the ride in this simulator almost like you are really in the plane. It will be as close to the real thing as we can get," she said.

"Will I feel the G-forces in turns and stuff?" I asked.

"In shallow turns you'll feel some movement of the simulator, and in violent movements you'll feel quite a lot. The images you see will trick your brain. You will actually feel like you're flying. But you won't feel the force of a six-G turn, or anything like that," Ms. Kraft explained.

"Now sit tight for a few minutes while we link up with the fighters out there."

I studied the gauges, dials, and switches. Some were familiar; some were just a mystery to me.

In a little while, Ms. Kraft came back.

"Okay," she said, "We're all set for the mission. I'm going to close the hatch, and what you'll see is a dull blue hue all around the inside of the canopy. Kind of like being inside a planetarium with the lights on low.

"Once we get switched into our real-time mode, you'll be linked through the high-speed computers, our communication system, and the video network to the fighters on the flight line. The pilots on the tarmac are going through their preflight checks now."

"Several final instructions for you, Andy. Your controls will not be active. That is to say if you touch any of these controls or gauges, nothing will happen to the real aircraft. We can control that and hook you up, or the pilot can hook you in if he chooses."

"What if I touch the stick?" I asked.

Ms. Kraft said, "That's no problem. In fact, you can follow through all the stick and rudder action. I'll set the link-up so that the controls in the simulator move in relation to the pilot's input in the real F-15. But your inputs will have no effect on the plane that's up there unless the pilot chooses otherwise."

I said, "Understood."

"Good," Ms. Kraft responded. "Second, communication is vitally important. Limit your conversation, but make sure you speak clearly. The computer hears and understands what you say, and you can control the entire aircraft with your voice. Also, the pilot in the plane needs to hear from you clearly. He wants to know what you are thinking or what you want him to do. So speak clearly and try to be short and crisp in your speech."

"You mean if I say turn left, the computer will turn left?" I asked.

I could hear Ms. Kraft chuckling. "No, Andy. The computer won't turn left. It's attached to the floor. But if you tell the computer, 'Left 60, go guns,' the aircraft will turn 60 degrees from your present heading and link up your cannon to the firing trigger on your stick. If you say, 'go auto land,' the computer will take over flying the aircraft and actually land it automatically."

"Will my guns be active?" I asked, amazed.

"Actually, the guns in the aircraft will be loaded, but your voice commands won't activate it," Ms. Kraft said. "You won't have control over any of the weapons systems."

This made sense, of course, but I couldn't help feeling a little disappointed.

"Third, Andy, if you are feeling any discomfort, let us know," said Ms. Kraft.

I asked, "You mean if I'm feeling air sick or something like that?"

"Right," she said. "Just say something, and we'll stop the activity and give you a break."

No way I'm gonna take a break, I thought. This is way too cool.

"You'll be linked to Captain Murdoch, flying wing for your dad and Captain Bonner," said the colonel. "Your flight is designated Cobra flight. Your dad and Snake are Cobra One. You and Mudhole Murdoch are Cobra two."

"Affirmative. Why the name Cobra?" I asked.

"Often we let the pilot flying lead chose the flight name designator," said the colonel. "Captain Bonner likes to pick names of different types of snakes. In this case, he chose Cobra as his designator.

"I'll be watching the action at the master control console with Ms. Kraft, Andy," Colonel Doctor said. "Have fun, guy. And keep your eyes open!"

"You bet!" I told him.

"By the way, Andy," said Ms. Kraft, "If you see something out there and you want to examine it more closely, you can ask the computer to 'stop action' and 'zoom image' accordingly. The computer will understand much of your commands if they are simple and direct."

"Understood," I said through the helmet.

Ms. Kraft stepped away from the cockpit and the canopy closed automatically.

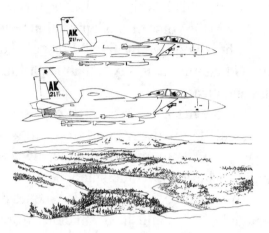

10
Recon

I kept looking over the gauges, trying to memorize the location of the important ones for flying.

"Andy," said the colonel over my earphones. He was speaking to me from the other simulator. "The fighters will be with us in a minute or two. Captain Murdoch will be calling you soon. Remember, he's call sign Cobra Two."

After a couple of more minutes, the visuals started to change. I could now see the runway at Elmendorf. It was surreal—almost real, but not quite. It was a mixture of video and enhanced computer graphics. The colors seemed more vivid than real life. Objects seemed just a bit fuzzy.

"Andy, this is Captain Murdoch. How do you read?" said the voice through my helmet earphones.

"I hear you five by five," I responded, just as Dad had taught me to say. That meant I heard him loud and clear.

"Andy, if I want to talk to you," said Captain Murdoch, "I will always start by saying 'Andy'. If you want to communicate with me, always start by saying, 'Murdoch.' Understand?" he asked.

"Affirmative," I responded. "Should I call you, 'Mudhole'?" I could hear chuckles from several voices over my headphones.

"Ah, Andy, that's O.K. You just call me Murdoch and we will get along fine. Understand?" asked Murdoch.

"Affirmative," I said. Again I heard chuckles through the headset. Obviously, the others listening knew something about the name 'Mudhole' that I didn't know. I wondered how a jet jockey would get the call sign 'Mudhole'. Too busy to worry about that now.

"Andy," said The Snake, "pilots usually will not speak during runup and take off. Normal procedure is to use hand signals. Today, though, we are going to use verbal communication in addition to our hand signals."

"Okay. We've completed our preflight checks. Two's ready," said Captain Murdoch over his intercom.

I looked to my left and could see the other F-15 aircraft, the one with Captain Bonner and my dad in it. Dad gave us a thumbs up from the back seat.

"One's ready," responded Captain Bonner from the other jet. "Elmendorf tower, Cobra flight of two ready for departure."

"Cobra flight of two, you are cleared for take-off," responded the tower controller.

Both aircraft taxied into position on the runway. I could see Captain Bonner's plane just forward and to our left.

"Combat take off roll on my mark," said Captain Bonner over the intercom.

"Two," responded Captain Murdoch.

"Power coming up now," said Captain Bonner.

"Two."

"Break release now."

"Two released."

We started to accelerate down the runway. Yellow lights on the edges of my visor lit up and moved slightly as our speed increased. They turned green when we reached flying speed, and continued to climb as we accelerated.

The simulator rocked back a little, and a quiet rumble sounded behind my head. Takeoff! I felt the stick and rudders move as Captain Murdoch's fighter climbed. Cobra One was now forward of us about 100 feet and climbing straight ahead.

"Climbing to level two two zero and coming left to heading one two zero," said Captain Bonner. That meant we were climbing to 22,000 feet and turning to a magnetic compass heading of one hundred and twenty degrees, roughly southeast.

"Two," I heard Murdoch say.

"Mark," said Bonner

"Two," replied Murdoch.

Both planes entered a gentle left climbing turn, passed through six thousand feet, and headed for Prince William Sound.

"Andy," said Captain Murdoch. "We'll climb to twenty-two thousand feet and stay there for the 20 minutes it will take us to reach the part of the sound where your Dad thinks this ship is located. Until we get there, I'll take up a position about a mile off the Snake's wing."

"Murdoch, how long will this take?" I asked.

"We're carrying about one and a half hours of fuel on board," said Murdoch, "so we'll have maybe 30 minutes to loiter out there before we need to head back. We'll take pictures and do some radar scans from high altitude because our engines are more efficient at altitude. If we see anything interesting, we'll go down and have a look. Understand, Andy?" he asked.

"Affirmative," I said.

I felt like I was really flying. As the two jets climbed in formation to their assigned altitude, I felt the sensations of the engines and the gentle rocking of the aircraft as it hit small pockets of unstable air. Our airspeed was climbing past 400 knots, or about 460 miles per hour. Aircraft, like ships, use knots instead of miles per hour. One knot per hour equals about 1.1 miles per hour.

Looking east, the Chugach Mountains stretched as far as I could see. In the distance, I could just make out the western shores of Prince William Sound, its fjords and glaciers coming into view over the nose of the aircraft.

"Go recon spread," said Cobra One.

"Two," replied Murdoch.

Captain Murdoch made a shallow turn to the south, and took up a parallel track to Cobra One about a mile off his right wing. I could turn my head to the left and see the jet carrying Capt. Bonner and my dad in the distance.

"Andy," said Captain Murdoch, "We are going to cruise for about 15 more minutes before we reach the position where we'll start our recon. Your dad says you've got flight experience. Why don't you take the stick and fly her for a while."

"Murdoch, are you serious?"

"Sure. Flying's flying. Are you game?"

"Okay!" I said. "I mean affirmative." Wow! I thought I was just going along for the ride. I never dreamed they would let me fly.

"We want to keep a heading of one two zero. That's one hundred and twenty degrees on the compass," said Captain Murdoch. "Our altitude is now one five thousand and climbing to twenty-two thousand. Shake the stick slightly when you have control."

I gently put my fingers around the flight stick and gave it a shake.

"Easy, Andy," said Captain Murdoch. "Flying this bird takes a very soft touch. It's both a hydro-mechanical and a fly-by-wire system, which means that the stick is linked to a computer, and the computer tells the other flight controls what to do. Be very gentle."

"Roger on all that," I said. My hands were perspiring, and I tried to be easy on the flight controls. My grip got tighter and tighter, and the jet started to climb too rapidly. I pushed the stick forward, and then we started down.

"Andy, relax your grip and try again. Just let go for a second and take a breath," said Captain Murdoch.

My hands were sweaty and I wiped them on my pants. I took a deep breath and tried to concentrate.

"Just because it doesn't work the first time," I could almost hear my dad saying, "don't give up. It takes a lot of practice and patience to learn something new. You won't get it right the first time. Sometimes you won't understand the concept until you just 'feel' what is the right thing to do.

"The root of all strength comes from knowledge. Knowledge comes from experience and understanding. And that comes from practice and more practice and learning from your mistakes. Keep trying, Bud, and never give up. Ever."

I tried again. This time, I was gentle on the control stick. I tried gently rocking the wings back and forth, in a shallow climbing bank from side to side.

"That's much better, Andy," said Captain Murdoch. "Now try a gentle 15-degree banked turn to the right and then turn back to our assigned heading."

I followed his directions and turned the jet into a 15-degree bank to the right. After completing that I started another 15-degree turn to the left, back to heading 120. I could read from the gauges in front of me that our speed was now 525 knots: almost 600 miles per hour.

"Andy, get ready to level her out," said Captain Murdoch.

We were approaching twenty-two thousand feet. Dad taught me that it was important to start leveling out a little before you reached the target altitude. But in a jet traveling at over 500 knots, I didn't quite know when to start the maneuver. I decided about 250 feet would be a good lead, so I started to push the plane's nose over just 250 feet shy of twenty-two thousand. I missed twenty-two by a few hundred feet, but quickly brought the plane back down to the assigned altitude.

"Andy, you're doing fine. Now hold her straight and level for a bit," said Captain Murdoch.

"Affirmative," I said.

"Cobra Two, this is Cobra One," said Captain Bonner. "Take up a cap at the KEBAB intersection. Fly your outbound heading of one six zero degrees for thirty miles, left turns, and scan."

"Two," said Captain Murdoch.

"Andy, we are on a heading to intercept the KEBAB intersection which is off the Johnstone Point VORTAC. When we reach the intersection, we'll make a right turn to a heading of one six zero. Copy all that?"

"Affirmative." The navigation equipment in the F-15 was similar to the gear Dad had on the Cessna 185. We'd often flown in instrument conditions. I understood that the KEBAB intersection was the intersection of two radio airways, kind of like a highway intersection. The Johnstone Point VORTAC was a radio beacon which broadcast the airways. It was located at Johnstone Point. I knew that Captain Murdoch was saying fly to that intersection and then fly an oval-shaped, racetrack pattern starting at the intersection. We would turn to a heading of 160 degrees at the KEBAB intersection and fly the racetrack pattern, making all left turns. This would bring us back to the KEBAB intersection.

Captain Murdoch was going to let me fly the intercept, pick up the outbound heading from the KEBAB intersection, and then start the oval-shaped, race track pattern that was part of Cobra Two's recon assignment.

"Murdoch," I asked, "how many circuits of the recon pattern will we fly?"

"Two," he replied.

"Andy, our radar will track various air and sea traffic in the sound, and the computers will record everything. We'll have a permanent record of all traffic in the area, especially the ships. After we're done with our scan, we'll join up with your dad and the Snake on a lower level recon of the various ships we spot from up here."

It was pretty simple flying the racetrack patterns. The challenge was to hit the KEBAB intersection each time. It took us about eight minutes to fly each circuit. I was so busy concentrating on flying the plane, that I had forgotten about Mitchey. Suddenly I remembered what I was up here to do.

"Cobra One, Cobra Two," said Captain Murdoch.

"Cobra Two, go ahead."

"I've identified what appear to be eight large ships in the sound," said Murdoch. "All of them seem to be moving, but it's tough to really tell from our equipment. The computer will be able to tell after our second scan. Position data is ready to be transferred to your flight computer." Captain Murdoch must be able to transfer his radar sightings to Cobra One's tracking computers, I thought.

"One's ready."

After about two minutes, we heard "Cobra Two, Cobra One will investigate the five targets to the east.

When your recon is complete, have a look at the three targets to the west."

The relative locations of the targets were displayed inside my helmet. There was also course and distance information to the closest target.

"Andy, when you've completed your second circuit, I'll take the stick," said Captain Murdoch.

"Affirmative."

I completed the second circuit about five minutes later and felt a gentle shake on the stick. I let go a little reluctantly.

"Hang on, Andy," said Captain Murdoch. I heard him chuckle.

The world went upside-down.

Captain Murdoch did a very rapid, 180-degree roll and pulled back on the stick. We had rolled inverted, were upside down and looking at the ground and water instead of the sky. I felt Murdoch pull back on the control stick, and the jet fighter started a dive towards the water below.

Our speed climbed past 600 knots as we headed for the surface. We were heading nearly straight down. At about 11,000 feet above the ocean, Captain Murdoch pulled back on the stick again, and the jet fighter began to level out at about 5,000 feet. We were heading straight toward the first ship on our recon mission.

"Andy, you still with me?" asked Captain Murdoch.

"That was way cool," I said. "Let's do it again!"

"I thought you might like that inverted dive," Captain Murdoch said. "We'll reduce power, and I'll be turning on our high-speed cameras as we pass over the ships we need to recon. You look for anything that seems unusual with those ships, or anything unusual on the ground or in the water. We need your eyes on this trip, so I'll fly and you look."

"Affirmative," I said, just a bit disappointed that the recon was taking center stage over the flying.

I'd seen pictures of cruise ships, but I'd never actually been on one, so I wasn't quite sure what to look for. But Dad always said look for something out of the ordinary, and trust your sixth sense. So I just started looking for anything that looked out of place.

We passed over the first ship, an oil tanker, just west of Valdez. It was headed south pushing a big wake, probably full of oil. Our first pass was at about 5,000 feet. As we came around for our second pass, Captain Murdoch dropped the F-15 down to about 500 feet above the water.

The water on Prince William Sound was calm, and there was an occasional iceberg floating near the beaches. Captain Murdoch passed over the ship, and people on the deck waved to us. The computer identified the ship as the *Exxon Long Beach,* out of Long Beach, California to Valdez and return, and displayed the information in the lower part of my helmet visor.

This computer is pretty amazing, I thought. It must link up with other databases so that it can even identify the names of ships and where they're from.

The computer gave us a course heading and distance to the next target, also an oil tanker. But this one was clearly inbound to Valdez. It was riding much higher in the water than the *Exxon Long Beach* and the computer identified it as the *ARCO Prudhoe Bay*, out of San Francisco. Nothing unusual there.

We headed toward our last recon target, a cruise ship. The ship was heading southeast toward open water. We approached from an initial altitude of about 3,000 feet.

"Cameras on," said Captain Murdoch.

"Murdoch," I said frustrated, "It's hard to get a good look at this speed."

"That's right, Andy. Just do the best you can," he said. "The camera records we're storing in the computer will let us study these ships in detail later on."

"But won't that take forever?" I asked.

"It takes a while to do good recon, but our specialists are the best there are. They work pretty quick."

We completed our first pass, and then headed back at a lower altitude for one more.

"Murdoch, there are lots of people on deck watching us. Mitchey said the ship she passed didn't have many passengers on deck."

The computer identified this ship as the *Princess Margaret*, out of Vancouver, British Columbia.

We pulled up after the second pass. I was disappointed we hadn't found the ship that—I just knew—had played a part in Mitchey's kidnapping. Thinking about what might be happening to her sent shivers up my body.

"Cobra One, Cobra Two, recon completed," said Captain Murdoch.

"Cobra Two, recon the last boat, about fifteen east of your present position."

"Two."

Captain Murdoch turned right and headed east toward the last ship. It was in international waters.

We flew east over the Gulf of Alaska and the seas were much heavier than in the sound. Our first pass of the ship was at about 3,000 feet. There weren't many people on the deck, but that might have been due to the heavy seas. The computer identified the ship as the *SS Finnlandia*, out of Vancouver, B.C. Our second pass was also uneventful, except not many people showed up on deck to see our pass. In fact, virtually no one showed up on deck. I felt let down that our recon hadn't produced the bad guys. Then I had a thought.

"Murdoch, can you figure out where that ship came from based on its present course?" I asked.

"I think we can make a reasonable estimate, based on its present course, assuming it hasn't made many turns. But our fuel is going to get critical in about five minutes, so we'll have to head back pretty soon."

"Cobra One copies that, Two," said Captain Bonner, meaning that both F-15's would need to head back to Elmendorf pretty soon.

"Andy, what are you thinking?" asked the Witch from the other simulator.

"Mitchey said that it seemed odd that a cruise ship didn't have many passengers on deck when she made her pass. The same thing just happened to us," I said over the intercom.

"She also thought that the ship was at anchor in a bay. The way I figure it, if that ship was involved in something illegal, and was trying to make a break for international waters, that it would take a direct route. So if we can plot its course in reverse, we might be able to find the general area where it came from," I explained.

"What have you got, Murdoch?" said the Colonel.

"Okay, Colonel," Murdoch said after a brief pause, "that ship might have been in the area of Zaikof Point on the tip of Montague Island. That's on our way back. Want us to take a look?"

"Affirmative, Murdoch," said the Colonel. "But don't get stuck in the mud."

"Yessir, there, Doctor Witch, I'll do my best to keep the wheels clean," replied Murdoch.

Again, there were chuckles of laughter over my headset.

The F-15 piloted by Murdoch now turned back northwest towards Montague Island. It was getting late, and the evening Alaska sun was getting lower on the horizon, but the light was still good. We approached the island from the southeast, and I could see a large bay just off to our left. It seemed in about the right spot from what Mitchey had said.

"Murdoch," I said, "can you fly low over the bay that is just west of Zaikof Point?"

"Affirmative. Do you want cameras rolling?"

"Affirmative," I replied.

We swung around the north tip of the bay and proceeded up the fjord. The bay is about five miles long, open to the north, and well protected from the ocean wind and waves. It's bordered by peaks on the east and south that rise up several thousands of feet. The peaks still had snow on them.

"Usually the weather out here is marginal," said Captain Murdoch. "But this is great visibility for recon. I won't be able to get very low in this particular fighter because of the higher terrain at the head of the bay, Andy. I hope the cameras do the trick for whatever it is you're looking for."

We turned south into Montague Bay.

I strained with my eyes to pick up something, anything, that might give us a clue. But the only objects visible on the bay were the little orange marking buoys fisherman use to mark their nets and crab pots.

Only the color of the water was strange in several places. Was it shallow, I wondered?

Between two buoys at the head of the bay the water was darker than the surrounding water. That's odd, I thought to myself. But at over 500 knots it was really tough to concentrate on one spot.

"Murdoch, can you go back to the head of the bay and make a pass over those buoys?" I asked.

"That will be about it, Andy. Then we'll have to head back," said Captain Murdoch.

He pulled the F-15 into a steep climb and then did a quick 180-degree turn back north towards the bay opening.

"Would it be too much to ask you to roll inverted? It will give me a clearer view of the water," I said.

"You do love this upside-down stuff, don't you?" Murdoch said.

"Okay, Andy, here we go. Look fast," said the fighter jock as he inverted the big twin-tailed aircraft.

After about five seconds I said, "Computer, freeze image," just like the colonel had told me. Everything just stopped.

"Andy, are we done now?" asked Captain Murdoch.

"Oh yeah, sorry, you can turn her back over. Sorry." I said. I felt the plane roll back over but the image of the water was still frozen over my head. I was looking up at the ocean. It was like a new kind of sky. I studied the image.

"Computer, four times zoom centered on the light area in the lower left center," I said. The computer zoomed in as I commanded. The dark area seems rectangular. About 100 yards long, and maybe 30 yards wide. If it was a sand bar, I thought, it shouldn't have a distinct shape like that. Pretty weird.

"What could it be?" I said aloud.

We were only about five minutes out from landing when Captain Murdoch called me.

"Andy," said Captain Murdoch, "follow me through the landing process. When I tell you to, tell the computer, 'gear down.' It will automatically extend the landing gear. Understand?"

"Affirmative," I said.

"You'll see three green lights in your helmet, in the shape of a triangle. That will confirm gear down and locked."

"I understand, Cobra Two," I replied.

Different lines and symbols appeared on my visor as Captain Murdoch guided the F-15 back for landing. They looked like part of the navigation system.

Another few seconds went by, and the tower cleared Cobra flight of two for a visual to runway zero six at Elmendorf. The jet banked right, then did a fly-by over the air field at about 2,000 feet. It banked hard left into a 180-degree turn and entered its downwind leg.

"Andy, this is how we lose speed rapidly," said Captain Murdoch as he pulled the nose up slightly and entered a hard descending left bank and final turn for the runway.

"Andy, gear down."

"Computer, gear down," I said. I heard and felt a quick thump/thud. Three green lights in a triangle shape appeared in my helmet.

"Gear down and locked, landing check satisfactory," said a pleasant voice in my helmet. The computer was talking to me!

I followed Murdoch's inputs to the control stick as he landed the F-15. What a sled ride!

Ms. Kraft opened the door to the simulator and began to unhook me from the virtual reality system.

"That was incredible!" I exclaimed as she helped me take off the helmet. "It was way too cool. I can't wait to tell the kids in Girdwood about this! That was the best thing I have ever done in my whole life." Well, it certainly ranked up there, anyway.

"Andy, good work," said the colonel, coming over from the other simulator. "You've been a big help. Whatever you and Murdoch found out there is more than your dad had coming in here. It may not be anything, but then again, it might be something. Our technicians are looking at that image right now. Unfortunately, our radar can't penetrate more than a couple of feet of the water surface, so if there is something there, the Coast Guard will have to confirm it."

"In the meantime, they'll use computer enhancement, combining the radar images and the visual images, and see if we can get a three-dimensional image of what might be there. It may just be a rock formation or a sand bar.

"Could it be something man-made?" I asked.

"Maybe we can tell, maybe we can't. But that is what recon is all about. Investigation and analysis," he said as we went back to the ready room to wait for Dad.

11
Debrief

There was a large table cluttered with several telephones and surrounded by plenty of chairs in the small conference room next to the pilot's ready room. Colonel Doctor motioned for me to sit down. I looked around. On one wall hung a whiteboard; pictures of various U.S. and foreign aircraft hung on the others. A large-screen television sat on a rolling cart and trailed lots of electronic cables that disappeared into the walls. The colonel picked up a VCR-type control that was also hooked to the wall.

"This control is linked back to our computer imaging system," he said. "The technicians are setting up all the footage the pilots took up there and are running it through an enhancement program. When the others get back, we'll run it and see if there's anything that'll help us.

"How about a soda?" he asked, pulling a Coke from a refrigerator hidden inside a wall cabinet.

"Thanks," I said, "I'm kind of thirsty."

The colonel slide it across the table.

Just about then, Dad and Captains Murdoch and Bonner came in.

Captain Murdoch went over to the refrigerator and pulled out a couple of sodas for the others.

"Witch," said Dad, "I owe you one. This is a tough situation, and your quick response appears to be moving our investigation along."

"Cowboy, we're glad to do it," said the colonel. "Just remember, you owe me a high-speed ski lesson this winter."

"That," said Dad with a grin, "is easily arranged."

Captain Murdoch sat down, and the colonel began the debriefing.

"First off, let's go around the room and see what each of you knows, thinks, or saw out there," he said.

We went around the table but no one had seen anything out of the ordinary, except for me.

"Let's have a look at the footage of that last ship Murdoch and Andy reconned, the *SS Finnlandia*. Then let's go back and see if we can make out anything from our visuals of Montague Island," said the colonel.

The colonel fast-forwarded the video tape to the *Finnlandia*, then slowed the tape down. We all scanned the ship.

Finally the colonel said, "Other than the lack of people on deck, the only thing that seems unusual are those lines running down the stern of the ship. See them?"

"Could they be a big set of doors, like cargo doors?" asked Snake Bonner.

"Can we get an image enhancement on that, Witch?" asked my dad.

"No problem," came the colonel's reply.

We studied the image for a few moments.

"It is really hard to tell," I said.

"If those were cargo doors, do you suppose an airplane could be loaded through those doors?" asked Dad.

"Plane might fit," said the colonel. "You said the plane spotted in Valdez was an amphib, right?"

Dad nodded.

"So it could land behind the ship and taxi right in," said Captain Murdoch.

"That could be our ship," said Dad. "But it's in international waters, so we can't touch it."

"And we still don't have any reason to," said the colonel.

"We don't know if they plan to come back, either," said Dad.

Captain Bonner said, "Maybe your lady friend spooked them so they pulled out early. If they left their work unfinished, they might come back."

"If they have to come back," I said, "maybe they're holding onto Mitchey as a hostage, just in case."

"Let's hope so, pal," said Dad.

"What I want to know is why hasn't this operation, or whatever it is, been discovered by the Coast Guard, or some other patrolling body?" asked Bonner.

"Maybe they disguise themselves as a cruise ship out of Vancouver," said Captain Murdoch. "They plan their schedule so that they arrive at that bay only when it's dark. They do their work, or research, or whatever, then get back underway to Vancouver at first light. Don't cruise ships make those kind of round trips, Armstrong? Just leave

Vancouver and never stop anywhere?"

"Well, it would be pretty unusual. After all, tourists come to see the sights, not just to spend the night. And what could they accomplish in just a few hours anchored in that bay? Overnight really isn't much time to do a whole heck of a lot of work," said Dad.

"If that's a support ship, maybe they just drop off supplies," said Captain Murdoch. "Or maybe they're just collecting research data. Or maybe they're after something that's so valuable that they need only a little bit to make it worth their work."

"That last is what my gut is telling me," said Dad. "People don't usually resort to kidnapping and attempted murder for research data.

"Witch, can you estimate their speed?" Dad asked.

"The computer is meant to deal with aircraft traveling at much higher velocities, but let's have a go at it," the colonel said. He punched a few buttons on his controller, and we saw numbers flash across the side of the TV screen.

"Looks like it's traveling at about 11 knots," he said.

"Hmm," said Dad. "Most ships usually travel about 16 to 19 knots. How accurate is that estimate?"

"It could be off by five knots," said Colonel
Doctor.

Captain Bonner spoke up again. "So maybe
they hightailed it out of town and are just hanging
out in international waters until nightfall. Then
maybe they'll go back to the bay."

"Too bad your computer can't read minds,
Witch," said Dad.

"We're working on that, too," said the colonel, and grinned. "Let's take a look at that bay your
boy spotted."

While the colonel was advancing to the next
set of images, Captain Bonner said, "There may be
another reason that ship is waiting out there in international waters."

"Why?" I asked.

"When I got our weather brief before the flight,
I saw that a storm is moving into the area later this
evening," he said. "A ship that size might be safer
in open seas than locked in some bay."

"When is the storm expected to subside?" Dad
asked.

"Probably by tomorrow midday," said Bonner.

"So what do you think?" asked the colonel as
the image of the bay came onto the screen.

"It's hard to tell, really," said Captain Murdoch,
after a few minutes. "Because the surface there is

darker than the surrounding areas, it looks like there should be deeper water there. But according to the navigation charts of the bay, it's not deeper. One thing's for sure. Something doesn't fit."

"What can your computers do with that contrasting lightness and darkness in the bay?" asked Dad.

"We've run several scans," said the colonel. "We've tried to build a 3-D image of what's under the water. Unfortunately about the only thing we've found is that the water temperature around the dark area is slightly warmer than the surrounding water."

"Could something under the water be giving off heat?" I asked.

"It could just be that the darker area absorbs heat during the day," said Dad. "Or you may be right. The heat source could be something like an underwater hot spring." He turned to the colonel. "Can you tell if that's a sand bar or something natural?" he asked.

"Not at this time," said the colonel. "Coastal geology is beyond what this system was designed to investigate. But my technicians are going to work on it. They have some geologist buddies over at the oil company, and they're going to try to put together our software with their databases. Unfortunately, that will take quite a bit of time to do."

"How much time?" asked Dad.

"Probably have some results tomorrow afternoon," said the colonel.

"Well," said Dad, "That's a long time. I guess we can only hope that the ship has unfinished business in the bay and is just waiting out the storm."

"What if it doesn't come back?" I asked.

"Then we get hold of Canadian customs and tell them what we suspect," said Dad.

"But I suspect that the ship made a run for it and that it is going to return to the bay," said Dad. "But it won't come back until after the storm subsides. It seems like our only lead in this case. Anyone else got ideas?"

The flyers looked at each other and generally agreed they couldn't contribute any more to the mystery.

"Well, doesn't seem like there's much else to talk about," Dad said. "And it's getting pretty late."

We got up and said our thank-yous and good-byes all around, and the colonel escorted us out to our car.

"I'll call you as soon as we have something more, maybe from the oil company," said Colonel Doctor as we approached Dad's patrol car.

"Thanks again, Witch, for all your help," said Dad.

"And thanks for the great ride!" I said.

"You bet, Andy. We'll see you again. Maybe someday for a real ride," the colonel said.

"*Yes!*" I shouted as we got into the car.

"Andy," said Dad, as we drove away from the air base, "I'm taking you home to bed, and then I've got some questions to ask of some friends down in Seward. I'll leave one of the deputies at the house. So you'll be okay."

I wondered why he would drive the 50 miles south to Seward rather than make some phone calls, but before I could ask him, I was asleep.

12
Late Night in Seward

Dad woke me when we got home and helped me to bed. I fell back to sleep so fast I didn't even hear him go out and the deputy come in.

So I almost fainted when I walked into the kitchen the next morning.

"Mitchey!" I shouted. "Am I glad to see you!"

"I feel the same," she said.

"But what happened? How'd you find her, Dad?"

"Whoa! Slow down. Get your breakfast and I'll tell you."

I grabbed the cereal and milk and was at the table in about 30 seconds.

"Okay. I'm ready," I said.

"Well, you know, driving 50 miles to Seward is not a big deal, especially late at night and in the patrol car," Dad said. "It's a pretty straight shot, really. I just cruised right along. Got into Seward in just about an hour and went straight to the station. Deputy in charge told me that nothing out of the ordinary had happened all summer.

" 'Any planes landing in the bay in the last few days?' I asked him. He said they were short-staffed, what with the police chief being away, and he didn't pay much attention to activity on the bay.

" 'Why do you ask? And it is late at night for even you guys to be out,' he said.

"So I told him about Mitchey, and that red amphib, and the cruise ship.

" 'You better talk to Bill Bowers, the harbor master,' the deputy said. He called, but Bowers wasn't happy about getting out of bed. After the deputy told him it was about a possible kidnapping, though, Bowers agreed to meet me down at the harbor office. The sun had set below the mountains to the northwest, but it wasn't dark outside, at least not yet.

"I had some time to kill before Bowers would be down at the docks, so I went over to the Salty

Dawg lounge to see if any of the local sailors had noticed a strange cruise ship or a sea plane.

"That place is as bad as its name," said Dad. "One of those seedy, old, run-down taverns that every harbor seems to have buried away in some back alley. There were ancient-looking sea ropes, sea floats and nets, even an antique wooden steering wheel from some ship hanging from the walls and ceiling. The walls were made of weathered wood, and the lamps gave off a sick yellow glow.

"It was late, but the bar was just warming up. The music was loud, there was too much smoke in the air, and the bartender had the look of a thug. Looked like he'd just gotten off some old sailing ship running drugs or illegals from the far east back at the turn of the century."

I laughed.

"No kidding," Dad said. "He had a black eye patch over one eye, and huge Popeye-type forearms, and tattoos from his wrists to his shoulders."

"You're making this up," I said.

"Dead serious," said Dad. But I still wasn't sure I believed him.

"So I went over to the bar, and asked this scary-looking bartender about who might have ferried supplies out to a cruise ship anchored in the sound recently.

" 'Who wants to know?' he snarled at me.

"Now it was late, and I was tired. Mitchey was missing, and I was not a happy camper. So I just leaned across the bar and put my face in his and slammed my federal I.D. on the bar." Dad leaned toward me and gave me an imitation. "Everyone in the place just shut up.

" 'Friend,' I told him, 'and I use that term loosely—*I* want to know. Marshal Sam Armstrong,' I said, emphasizing the Marshal. 'Now I don't have a lot of time. If you waste any of it, I might be tempted to mess with you. And, you *don't* want that. So you want to help me?'

" 'Well, since you put it like that,' he said, and I noticed him slowly reach under the bar with one hand. I didn't like that much, so I reached over the bar, grabbed his wrist, and slammed it up into the underside of the bar. He yelled and dropped something."

" 'Back off, now,' I told him. He backed away and I went around the end of the bar. He'd dropped this long electrical cord with a button switch attached to the end.

" 'And where does that lead to?' I asked.

" 'Over here,' said a voice behind me.

" 'And you are?' I asked as I turned towards the voice.

" 'The owner. And *you* are?' When I told her she said, 'You're out of your jurisdiction. What do you want in my bar?'

" 'Questions answered,' I said.

" 'Well, let's not disturb the patrons, shall we?' she said. 'Step into my office and we'll discuss this.'

"Jan Cassidy was in her fifties. She was a bit overweight, and her skin was puffy. Probably because she sampled too much of her own booze. She wasn't short, especially; maybe about five foot five. Her hair was grey and blonde. I guessed she was a real stunner maybe twenty years ago.

"We went into her office, and she closed the door.

" 'I'm Jan Cassidy,' she said. 'Now, what do you want here?'

" 'A friend of mine was kidnapped early this morning,' I told her, and I emphasized the word 'friend.' 'The kidnappers almost got my son, too, and it is getting late. I am trying to find this person, and the kidnappers. So you can understand I might be a very unhappy person right now.' I told her.

"She kind of eyed me but I guess she figured she wouldn't mess with me. She nodded and said, 'It's a tough job, I guess.'

" 'I suspect the whole thing has something to

do with a large ship, maybe a tourist ship, that might be hanging around Montague Island in the Prince William Sound. What it might be doing there, I don't know. Have you heard any talk?' I reached in my pocket and pulled out a twenty-dollar bill and laid it on the table between us. Jan eyed the cash.

" 'Well, I did hear that a ship's been operating up near Montague Island,' she said. 'Supposed to be a cruise ship, but rumor has it that there aren't any tourist-type passengers on board. It is supposed to be doing some kind of research, which isn't unusual. After the big oil spill by Exxon a few years back, many ships do research. Some of their crew have been into town to pick up supplies. They stop in here for a quick one, you know, but they don't talk much.'

" 'Did they say what kind of research or for who?' I asked.

" 'They didn't say. The crew pretty much keeps to themselves when they are in here.'

" 'Nothing else, Jan?' I asked and kind of stared her down.

"She just stared back. 'No,' she said. 'Want me to ask around?'

"I told her to go ahead. But that proved to be a big mistake and a blessing!"

13

At the Seward Dock

When I left the bar, I drove down the dock straight to the harbor master's office. The office was in an old wooden building with square windows and a metal roof. Several doors seemed to be hung onto storage sheds. The main door was glass and wood. There was a flag pole in front of the ramshackle structure.

"Behind the office, the docks stretch along the shore line for almost a mile. To the south are the larger, commercial ships including the University of Alaska's new geographic explorer vessel. To the north are smaller ships— commercial fishing boats and privately-owned yachts.

"It was almost dark, and the docks are not well lit. The harbor master's office lights weren't on, but I walked over and tried the door anyway. It was locked. I could have forced it open easily, but that wasn't necessary because Bowers was on his way.

"Bowers hadn't arrived, yet. So I walked down towards the bigger ships, and leaned against the railing overlooking the wharf while I tried to figure out what really was going on in this cruise ship/kidnapping thing. What was this ship doing in the sound? What kind of research?

"The storm Captain Bonner told us about was approaching, and the weather was starting to turn bad. The wind was blowing at about 20 to 30 knots, and the seas were probably four to five feet high. Clouds were appearing over the southern sky and moving rapidly in the direction of the bay.

"I started to walk back toward the harbor master's office when I spotted a red amphib moored way out on the end of one of the docks. The light was low, and I was lucky to see it because it was well hidden between several large boats.

"A lightning bolt of excitement just shot through me. I got pretty excited. I had a feeling that this was the plane that had been involved in the kidnapping of Mitchey. The floating docks were pretty confusing, and I wasn't sure which ramp to take out to the plane.

"I had to pick my way past a row of buildings, mostly old wooden structures used by fisherman for cleaning and sorting bait. Then I found a ramp that looked like it would lead me to the plane. Just as I turned down it, I was grabbed from behind. Two huge, very strong, hands just grabbed my shoulders and lifted me off the ground. I was spun around and slammed against the railing.

"I only caught a glimpse of the men. There were three of them, all very tough. They looked like sailors, and I'm pretty sure they had military training from the way they fought.

"Three to one is a tough match, and I couldn't get the upper hand. Finally, the two larger guys had me held tightly by my arms and shoulders. One of them was hanging onto my hair. I was facing away from them and couldn't see their faces. I struggled some, but I felt one of them pull out a knife and jab it against my back. I felt him draw blood, so I figured I'd better cool it.

"The third man, who was clearly the leader, said, 'You been trying to find us, mister lawman. Unfortunately for you, we found you first. Since we can't take you with us, we'll just have to get rid of both you and the pretty lady.'

" 'They have Mitchey!' I thought. 'But where?'

"I tried to stay calm and buy some time," said Dad. "So I asked him, 'You gonna kill me right here? That would be awfully messy. You know I'm the law. You kill me and you got one big problem on your hands.'

"The leader sounded kind of doubtful, then he reached over and pulled my wallet out of my pocket.

" 'Yeah, you are the law,' he said. 'But that doesn't change things. We'll just take you and the lady for a little airplane ride. Too bad it'll be a one-way trip for you. Say, do you own a parachute? The water gets pretty firm without one.'

"The two guys holding me started shoving me down the walkway to the dock below. I still couldn't see their faces.

"Just then an old drunk stumbled around the corner of a nearby fish building. He had a cane, and was wearing a long coat that flapped in the breeze. He carried a brown paper sack probably containing a wine bottle.

"As the poor old guy stumbled straight toward us, the ringleader shouted at him, 'Get your butt out of here, you old drunk.'

"The drunk seemed not to hear. The drunk was almost next to the one who seemed in charge. The ringleader started to yell again, when the old man lifted his cane and whacked the ringleader hard— and I mean really hard!—across the chest and shoulder. The ringleader went down with a crash.

"The other two were pretty surprised and one of them started to let go of me. I wasn't going to miss this opportunity.

"I kicked free of the two guys holding me, and came out fighting. I realized that the old drunk was swinging his cane. Unfortunately, his best blow was the first one he landed on the pilot's chest. But he did get in some good licks and improved my odds.

"When one of the big guys went down, I saw the leader get up and run down the dock. The old drunk, who obviously wasn't drunk—grabbed some rope from somewhere and tied the one guy up. I finished off the other guy and looked over at my new friend.

" 'Can you take care of this one, too?' I asked.

" 'I'm fine,' he said. 'Go after the other guy.'

"I raced down the dock. The leader was casting the seaplane off from its moorings. As I sprinted toward him, he moved around to the cockpit side of the airplane.

"The plane started floating out into one of the small channels between two main piers of moored boats. I was running hard, but the plane was slipping away. As I reached the end of the dock, the amphib began to taxi around the end of the main pier.

"Well, that gap between me and the plane looked awful big but there weren't any other choices. I pushed my running a little harder and leaped off the end of the dock toward the plane. I managed to grab one of the amphib handholds as I landed on the wing."

"Geez, Dad, you could have been hit by the prop!" I yelled.

"Don't think that didn't cross my mind," he said. "But that amphib was a Lake. The engine is on top of the fuselage and the propeller faces to the rear, a pusher-style prop. It pushes the plane through the air instead of pulling it like most prop/engine combinations. So when I jumped for the plane, I was out of the way of the turning prop.

"The storm was coming in so the pilot couldn't taxi out into the rough seas of the bay where the waves would have swamped him. He had to take off from the protected harbor. There was enough room in the harbor, but just barely. He had to get rid of me first, though. I was crawling across the wing, looking for the top hatch that opens into the cockpit.

"I managed to work my way up to the hatch. But as I started to turn the handle, the pilot started using engine power to try to buck me off while he tried to taxi the plane into position for take-off. I wasn't about to get bucked off. I didn't plan on getting sucked back into the prop. There were handholds all over the top side of that amphib.

"Just as I managed to unlock the hatch, up came the pilot. He'd left the plane's controls to idle in the harbor channel. He had to get rid of me if he was going to take off.

"He tried to beat me off with a long steel pole he pulled out from somewhere, and I almost lost my grip a couple of times. I had to hang on and could only fight him with one hand. He had both hands free but had to stand half in the plane.

"I finally got hold of the pole and dragged him farther out of the plane. He lost his balance and fought for a hand hold. I swung my leg around and knocked him out of the plane's cockpit. He was out of control."

Dad stopped for a minute. And I could almost see what had happened. Mitchey closed her eyes.

"He died instantly," said Dad. He took a sip of his coffee and the room was quiet for a while.

"Well," said Dad finally. "With no one at the controls, we were drifting and I could see we were heading into a boat nearby. I crawled into the cockpit and jumped forward into the pilot's seat. I pushed the throttle slightly forward and turned the control wheel and stomped full on the rudder pedal. We just missed the boat.

"Then," he said, "I realized I had a copilot."

14
Harbor Master's Office, Seward

Who wasn't much help," said Mitchey.

"You were on the plane the whole time!" I shouted.

"Yes, and I was really glad to see your dad. When he finally got the plane back to the slip and got me untied, I asked him, 'How'd you know I was here?'

" 'It was just luck,' he said. 'I had a hunch about Seward.'

" 'Well, I'm sure glad for your hunch, Sam,' I told him.

"What happened after they kidnapped you?" I asked her.

"They flew me to some remote lake in the mountains between here and Girdwood," she said. "They just taxied up on shore, hauled me out, and started questioning me. They were pretty rough."

"Is that where you got the black eye?" I asked.

"Yeah," she said. The thought of those guys beating up on her made me kind of sick. "I was lucky, though," said Mitchey. "They didn't break any bones. They just wanted to know what I knew and who I told. I think they would have killed me and dumped my body somewhere. But when I told them that Sam had called the Coast Guard and the F.A.A., they seemed unsure about what to do with me. So they tied me up and flew here to Seward. I heard them talking that they could find out more about Sam from their connections down there."

"What about the drunk?" I asked Dad. "Who was he?"

"Bill Bowers, the harbor master. He was just acting drunk," said Dad. "In fact, it turns out he was an ex-Marine. That's why he was so willing to wade into the fight.

"After Mitchey and I got out of the plane, Bill walked up, cool as you please, and said, 'I assume all of that has to do with why you rousted me out of my bed in the middle of the night?'

" 'It does,' I told him. I introduced Mitchey. 'She's the one who was kidnapped earlier today by those fellows.'

" 'Did you call the Valdez deputy by chance?' I asked him.

"He just jerked his thumb over his shoulder. It was then I noticed the lights of the patrol car pulling up by his office.

" 'Guess we got some talking to do,' I said, and the three of us headed toward the office."

"What did you learn from those guys?" I asked.

"Well, it's like I suspected," said Dad. "Two were just hired thugs. They really didn't know much. Just a couple of local criminals out to make a little Christmas money.

"We had them handcuffed and sitting in chairs in a corner of Bill's office," said Dad.

" 'What do you want me to book them for?' the deputy asked me.

" 'Assault, kidnapping, attempted murder. You know,' I said, 'the usual.'

" 'I still don't understand what this is all about,' said Bill. 'Mind bringing me up to speed?'

"So I gave him a quick rundown on what we'd learned.

" 'That plane has been in and out of here several times. I've seen it land,' said Bill when I'd finished. 'Nothing unusual about that. I figured it was probably picking up supplies of one kind or another.'

" 'But the *Finnlandia*, you say. We get a lot of cruise ships coming up from Vancouver.' He started looking through his log book and stacks of paperwork. 'We have several entries last year for the *Finnlandia*. As I recall, several of the local merchants complained that its passengers didn't seem to spend much money on trinkets and such.'

"I asked him, 'Would it be unusual for the ship to cruise up from Vancouver, and then cruise back without making any ports of call?'

" 'You mean it didn't stop anywhere?' asked Bill.

" 'Not as near as we can tell.'

" 'It's not unusual for a cruise ship to come up from B.C. and not make a final port call at the northern end of the journey,' Bill said. 'But it would be very weird for it not to make *any* port calls. That is part of a cruise to Alaska, stopping off and visiting places like Juneau, Sitka, and Skagway.'

" 'That's what we thought,' I told him. 'I'd sure give a lot to know what they're doing now.' "

"That's when I stopped acting like a bump on a log," said Mitchey. "After all, I'd spent quite a few hours with those thugs. And since they figured they were going to kill me anyway, they didn't bother keeping anything secret.

" 'I may be able to help you,' I told your dad. 'The guy who died radioed out from that Lake amphibian. Probably out to the ship. He asked for a rendezvous time. The response on the other end was that they needed to wait out the storm. They planned the rendezvous for tomorrow in the afternoon, about 1 p.m.'

"They hadn't said where they were going to meet," said Mitchey. "But we figured the bay at Montague."

"I also heard the men on the other end of the radio say that the pressure was increasing, and that this would be their last score. They said to leave all the gear. They'd made enough of a haul, and it was time to clear out. That was about it."

"But it was enough for me to realize that they were doing more out there than just researching valuable resources," said Dad.

"I'm sure they're after something worth a lot of money," said Mitchey.

Dad nodded.

"What happened then?" I asked.

"Not much," said Dad. "The deputy locked the guys up, called the Coast Guard station, and told them what we knew about the rendezvous time and probable location. Asked them to expedite a cutter to Montague and to expect trouble.

"But as the deputy was locking the two guys into the car, I had an idea.

" 'Bill,' I said, 'I have one more favor to ask.'

" 'Name it,' the harbor master said.

" 'Could you arrange to have that plane flown up to Girdwood when the storm passes? As early as possible tomorrow?'

" 'No problem, Marshal. I know a good pilot.' He gave me this narrow look. 'What are you plotting?'

" 'If they're expecting this plane tomorrow afternoon, we wouldn't want to disappoint them, now would we?' I told him.

"Bill laughed. 'You'll have the plane in Girdwood. I'll call your office when it takes off from here,' he said.

" 'What about that blood on your shirt, there, marshal?' asked Bill.

"I fingered where the knife had cut me. I pulled up my shirt and they could see the wound wasn't bad. I didn't think it would need stitches. Bill reached for his first aid kit and pulled out alcohol and swabs.

" 'I'll live, I suppose,' I said. Mitchey grabbed the alcohol and started cleaning up the mess on my backside.

" 'You know, Sam, you ought to have this checked by a doctor,' she said. 'It doesn't look bad, but then maybe it could get infected. And who knows where that knife has been.' And she rattled on about the wound. Mitchey was just taking her mind off the stress of events in her day." Dad looked over at Mitchey with a grin.

"Bill, the harbor master, was still chuckling when we left his office."

At that last comment, Mitchey scowled at Dad in a fun sort of way.

15
A Plan of Action

We were all kind of quiet for a minute when Dad finished his story. Mitchey stopped smiling all of a sudden, and gazed out the window. I guess she remembered what she'd been through, because I saw her shiver. Outside the wind was blowing pretty hard, and the rain was coming down at an angle. The predicted storm had finally hit, but it was supposed to pass through rapidly.

"So, what's our plan now?" I asked Dad in all seriousness.

"Our plan," he said, "is to keep you and Mitchey out of harm's way."

I frowned, and Mitchey didn't seem all that happy about it, either.

"So what's that supposed to mean?" I asked.

"This storm is supposed to blow out by noon. That's probably when the *Finnlandia* will head back to the bay to pick up whatever is there. Since they're expecting the amphib to meet them this afternoon, I'm going to fly it out there with Witch," said Dad.

"Then what're you going to do?" I asked.

"We really don't have anything on this ship. We don't really know that it's doing anything illegal. We need hard evidence," he said.

I was quick to interrupt. "Wait a minute. They tried to kill Mitchey two times, beat her up and beat up on you, too! Of course, they're doing illegal stuff! Mitchey even heard them talking about it on the radio," I said.

"All we have, Andy, are the guys who kidnapped Mitchey, and jumped me. Mitchey heard them radio to someone, but we can't prove it was someone on the ship. All we really have on the ship are our suspicions. Granted, we think we know what they're up to, but we have to move in and find out what is really going on.

"So you're just going to fly out there all alone, board the ship, and just look around?" I asked incredulously.

"I suspect your dad has it figured out a bit better than that," said Mitchey.

Dad smiled.

"The Coast Guard is sending over a cutter. They'll try to give us backup, but timing is important because the *Finnlandia* apparently is expecting to see the amphibian in the early afternoon.

"Mitchey, how much time do you have in a 185?" Dad asked.

"Probably 250 hours, and about 25 hours on instruments in the last five years," she replied.

"That will work," Dad replied. "I'd like you to fly over to Valdez in our 185.

"Andy, you can go along and work the radios. I want the two of you to man a radio relay station. The bay is far enough out in the gulf," he said, "that we might not have good line-of-sight radio broadcast capability. And from the ship, our FM transmissions probably won't reach farther than six or seven miles. You'll relay our transmissions to my office here in Girdwood and to the Coast Guard.

"I'll be using several frequencies to broadcast our progress. I've written them down on this notepad." Dad handed Mitchey a small, police-type notebook. "The 185 has several radios, so you'll be able to tune into the air-to-air and air-to-ground frequencies. I'll be broadcasting every five minutes, once we approach the ship.

"I want you to stay at a safe distance away from the bay. At least *five miles* away. Under *no* circumstances are you guys to come any closer than *five miles*. Understand?"

"You've got it, Captain," Mitchey said.

I saluted. "Yes, sir."

"Witch is driving down from Anchorage with a Coast Guard officer to give us a briefing on some information his people have pulled together," said Dad. "I'm going over to the office to meet him. I'll let you two put together some lunch and the stuff you'll need on the plane." He put the keys to the Jeep on the table. "Mitchey, you can drive the Jeep over when you've finished."

After he'd gone, I asked Mitchey, "How much food should we take?"

She laughed. "Worried about that famous hollow leg of yours?" she asked.

"Yeah, well," I said.

"We're going to be hungry," she said. "So let's take a good supply of food."

We started making sandwiches and I dragged out an old backpack to put the lunches into.

"What else do we need?" I asked her when we'd finished.

"Well, just in case, I'll take my survival bag," she said.

"What's in it?" I asked.

"Sleeping bag, food, water, a tent, change of clothes, rope, gloves, rain coat and hat, fishing pole, flares, knife, compass, flashlight and batteries, saw or ax, and a gun," she said.

"A *gun*?" I asked. "You carry a gun? Isn't that dangerous?"

"Guns *are* dangerous," she said. "And I don't like them. But a gun is an essential piece of survival equipment when you're flying in the back country. It could save your life. The noise it makes travels for many miles. It's much louder than your voice. You might need it for food, or for protection, especially if you're injured. I keep an unloaded gun in my survival bag, and the ammunition in a separate container in the same bag. I always keep the bag under my seat so I can reach it with one hand."

"Geez, that's a lot of stuff to carry," I said.

"Sounds like it, unless you just happen to need it," Mitchey said.

"Well," she said, as I tightened the straps on the backpack, "If you're all packed, let's go."

16
Briefing at Girdwood

When we got to Dad's office, everyone was already in the small conference room he also used for interrogations.

"Let's make introductions all around," said Dad. "This is my deputy, John Riley. Next to John is my son, Andy. This is Mitchey Peters. At the end of the table is Colonel Frank Doctor, and his aide, Captain Laura Smithson. She is an expert on geology and computer simulation. Finally, this is Commander Anne Priest of the Coast Guard. She flew up from Juneau this morning. Witch, go ahead."

"It's very nice to meet the person we thought we'd lost for good," said Colonel Doctor to Mitchey. He looked at Dad and said, "You were absolutely correct. She was worth saving. And she is a beauty." Everyone laughed including me. Mitchey blushed.

"Captain Smithson is our expert on computer generation and enhancement. I'm going to let her explain what we've found. Captain?"

"This slide projector has an adapter which allows us to display computer-generated images through the lenses," said Captain Smithson. "We have hooked it up to this portable computer which is linked through a high-speed communications modem to the oil company's super computer."

I knew that a modem was a device that let computers talk to each other through the phone lines.

"We used the super computer's imaging programs and stored files to enhance our recon data. Then we combined it with the data the oil companies use for exploration. Their systems, many of which are linked to satellites, allow them to 'see' beneath the surface of the earth. The systems are designed to estimate the probable location of oil and gas fields based on known relationships in geology and geography.

"In this first image, made about a year ago, you can see the area of Montague Bay. Now we overlay information about the geology of the region." She slipped a new slide into place. "Notice the fault line running through the bay.

"What's interesting is that when we looked at a broader area, we found that the fault line comes to the earth's surface only through the bay." The captain brought up another slide. "It disappears deep into the earth's crust on the east and west ends of the bay.

We also looked at the relative water temperatures for the bay and the surrounding Prince William Sound. The surface temperatures are similar, but about 200 feet down in the bay, the water temperature is significantly warmer than water of the same depth in the sound."

"Why is that?" I asked.

"The earth's crust is made of gigantic floating areas known as plates," said Captain Smithson, smiling at me. "In parts of the Pacific Ocean, all along what's called the Ring of Fire, the heavier oceanic plates are diving or subducting underneath the lighter continental plates. Great pressure, heat, and stress is created where the plates collide. When the plates actively slip, we feel the slippage as earthquakes. Alaska, of course, is a very active earthquake area.

"These geological faults are usually many thousands of feet deep. Molten rock from the earth's core can come close to the surface or even break through the surface along these faults. That's why we often see active volcanos and hot springs on or near them.

"Oceanographers and geologists have discovered that valuable minerals are often pushed up along these faults. One of the most important minerals discovered has been a nickel-molybdenum nodule, about the size of a basketball. This mineral combination is very rare, and is very valuable for certain types of military warfare. It can't be mined commercially, though, because it comes from so deep in the earth.

"We suspect," the captain continued, "that because of the unique geology of Montague Bay, that this and other minerals may be present in significant quantities. No one's had a reason to search here before but the sophisticated research tools now available to many countries might mean that someone has spotted the unusual warm spot in the bay."

"So the *Finnlandia* may be an active mining vessel," said Dad.

"Exactly," said Captain Smithson. "We went back and plotted the *Finnlandia's* radar track for the last 30 days. You can see in this sequence of radar plots," she brought up another slide, "that the ship made four trips to the bay from Vancouver. Each time it arrived, it stayed overnight, then departed the next day, moving off shore into international waters.

"We used our recon data and the oil company's computer programs to look at the bay's geological structure. We didn't find anything unusual, at first, and could not explain the dark spot Andy saw yesterday."

"After several enhancements to the photos and the computer-generated files, however, we found that the dark spot is an area of the sea floor which has been disturbed. Notice that in the photos taken a year ago there was no discoloration of the bay floor." She clicked to the next slide. "Now notice the same place yesterday." The image Captain Murdoch had made during recon came onto the screen. "Clearly a darker area," said Captain Smithson.

Commander Priest asked, "What are your conclusions?"

"We believe the floor of the bay contains valuable minerals," said Captain Smithson. "We think that the *Finnlandia* is illegally mining at night using some type of strip-mining device. The ship is certainly big enough to contain very sophisticated equipment."

"How sure are you of this?" asked Commander Priest.

"We are positive of the ship's movements," said the colonel. "We are not positive about the mineral extraction. It's our best guess." He turned to Dad and said, "But I'd bet a case of brewskis on it."

Dad laughed and said to Commander Priest, "I wouldn't bet against a case."

She smiled. "Do you know the location of the ship?" she asked. "Our radar doesn't have the range in that part of Alaska."

Dad said, "We are pretty sure the ship was planning to pick up the pilot of the red amphibian later today. We suspect the *Finnlandia* will make a run out of international waters later today when the storm subsides. She'll try to pick up the pilot and whatever goods they have cached or evidence they've left behind in the bay."

"Our nearest cutter is on the way, but it's still probably four hours from the bay," said Commander Priest, looking at her watch. "We can board and inspect the ship, but only once it is in U.S. waters. If the ship picks up its cargo and goes before we get there, there's nothing we can do."

"Witch and I have a plan to keep them around long enough for you to get the cavalry out there," said Dad. The colonel just rolled his eyes. The commander raised an eyebrow.

"We're going to fly the amphib out to the *Finnlandia*. We think the plane is either hoisted onto the ship, or taken in through a big set of doors in the stern. The crew of *Finnlandia* shouldn't suspect anything unusual until the seaplane is on board. We'll attempt to arrest those on board, and detain the ship long enough for the Coast Guard to get its cutter to the bay."

"Two of you against who knows how many people on board," said Commander Priest.

"Yes, but I'm the law and he's the military," said Dad. "We'll be carrying a federal warrant. Legally, we have the power to detain the ship."

"You're nuts," said the Commander. "You don't even know the layout of the ship."

"We've managed to get copies of the ship's engineering drawings," said the colonel.

"That ship's bound to have been highly modified since those drawings were done," said the commander.

"True," said the colonel, "but the basic layout should be the same."

"There's got to be a better plan" said the commander.

"If the information we have is correct," said

Dad, "that ship will pull in and out today. If we don't try to stop it, it will be in international waters before you can get there. If you have a better idea, I'm open to it."

"Unfortunately I don't," said Commander Priest. "But I still don't like this. How are you going to communicate with anyone, including us?" she asked.

"We'll have portable radios for communication. Actually, neck mikes attached to portable radios," said Dad. "Mitchey will be flying our 185 as a communications link to our base here and to the Coast Guard."

"Well, I'm still not happy about it," said Commander Priest. "But I guess I'd better get you the frequencies and the instructions you need. Where's the telephone?"

"This way," said Deputy Riley, and led her out of the room.

"Okay," said Dad to the rest of us. "We'll leave for Montague as soon as the rain stops and we have decent flying weather. Let's rendezvous at the airstrip pretty quickly."

17
Montague Bay

By lunch time the storm had lifted, the amphib had been delivered to Girdwood air strip, the Cessna had been loaded, Dad had given us our last-minute instructions, and we were airborne.

In the Lake amphib, Dad and the colonel were wearing voice-activated mikes around their necks so we could hear pretty much everything being said by them and by anyone near them. Dad's 185 had a cockpit recorder and he wanted us to record everything said on the way out to the *Finnlandia* and once they were on board.

Dad said they weren't sure what to expect out on the ship, but he told me that Colonel Doctor was one of the few Air Force officers trained for special types of assault operations. He didn't explain the details.

We expected to reach Montague Island in about thirty minutes. Mitchey flew the 185 smoothly, and I followed through on the controls.

"Dad usually lets me do the takeoffs," I told her. "but he hasn't let me really land this 185. He lets me follow through, though, on the controls. I'm pretty sure I could do it if I had to."

"Well, let's hope not today," said Mitchey. "Your job is the radios."

I had four radios to monitor. The ship-to-shore radio was tuned to the Coast Guard frequency and the police radio was tuned to Dad's portable radios. There were also two aircraft radios, one tuned to the air-to-air frequency, and the second tuned to a relay station connected to Elmendorf Air Force base operations. The colonel had said he wanted us to have that frequency "just in case." The SOFF or Supervisor of Flying, and the officer on duty in the Elmendorf command post had both been briefed on our activity, he said, and the base was properly alert.

"Cessna one eight five Alpha Juliet, how do you copy?" came Dad's call on the radio.

"Five Alpha Juliet copies five by five," I said.

"Five Alpha Juliet, why don't you fly off my left wing at about a quarter mile. We'll keep our altitude at about 500 feet, just in case the *Finnlandia* has radar that can detect airplanes. That altitude will mask us from her visual and electronic sights, because we'll be flying below the mountain ridges."

Mitchey nodded to show she'd heard and understood.

"Five Alpha Juliet copies," I replied.

"Sure seems odd to be looking at my own plane," I heard Dad say.

"It sure is a beautiful craft," said the colonel.

"Andy, do you copy our chatter?" asked Dad.

"That is affirmative," I said.

"Your kid sure is one smart boy," the colonel said.

"Yeah, I really am a lucky dad."

Mitchey and I smiled.

We flew on for the next thirty minutes through some spectacular fjords and glacier scenery. We didn't talk much, except for Dad's check-ins every five minutes. He wanted us to keep our radio chatter to a minimum.

As we approached Montague Island, Dad said, "Five Alpha Juliet, take up station."

I responded with two mike clicks. Mitchey climbed to 2,000 feet, just below the ridge line of the hills to the west of Montague Bay. Dad's plane descended and began an approach into the bay from the northwest. He was flying about 100 feet off the water. As soon as he turned into the bay around the ridge line, we lost sight of him.

"There's the *Finnlandia*," I heard Dad say. "Let's circle it and see if we can catch their attention."

"Oh, we'll get their attention since we don't know their radio frequency," said the colonel.

"Holy smokes!" The colonel interrupted himself. "Look at the stern of the ship. It's opening up, just splitting in half. So that *is* how they get the plane inside."

"What do you think, Witch?" Dad asked. "Can we make it?"

"It'll be close, but we should be able to taxi right inside the ship," said the colonel. "We may have problems with our radio transmission though once we're inside that steel beast. This is an amazing operation. Whatever they are searching for sure must be worth a lot of money.

"Quite a few people on deck," continued the colonel. "Now why is it, Cowboy, that people on the ground always have to wave at a plane? Rock your wings Marshal, as we go by. Then let's set her down and taxi up to the stern."

"Aye, aye, Captain," came Dad's response.

A few moments passed. I wondered if Mitchey was as tense as I was.

"Easy, easy!" came the colonel's voice. "Good landing, Cowboy."

"That open hull looks like a giant clam ready to gobble us up. It's almost scary," said Dad.

"Yeah, it is scary," said the Witch.

"Mitchey," I asked, "what if we lose their transmissions when they get inside that steel hull?"

"I'm not sure, Andy," said Mitchey. She looked troubled.

The ship-to-shore radio came alive.

"Bay Watch, this is Coast Guard cutter Resolute, how do you copy?" Bay Watch was our code name.

"Resolute, this is Bay Watch. We read you four by five. How far away are you?" Four by five meant we heard them pretty good, but not crystal clear over our radio.

"Bay Watch. Resolute is 75 miles southwest.

We should be on site in three hours. Say status,"
came the Coast Guard's response.

"Dad, I mean Marshal Armstrong, and his boarding party just landed next to the ship," I said. "They
said the back end opened up and they're taxiing in.
We can't see any activity from where we are stationed."

"Roger that, Bay Watch. Keep us posted.
Resolute clear."

"Bay Watch clear."

"I wish they were closer," said Mitchey.

Just then I picked up talk from Dad's plane
over the police band.

"Taxi in easy, Cowboy." I could hardly hear
the colonel's voice. "Okay, now shut down the engines. Wow, look at this thing. It's huge. Oh, oh,
Cowboy, we got trouble. They're closing the ship
doors behind us."

The transmission from Dad's plane started to
get garbled.

"... no ... cruise ship ..." said Dad or the colonel.
I couldn't distinguish their voices. "... mining gear
over there ... hoists set ... roof ... cargo
hold ... floor! ... opens up underwater."

"Mitchey," I said, getting scared for Dad, "I
can barely make out what they are saying."

"Keep listening, and I'll take us a little closer,"
she said.

"But Dad said to stay five miles away," I said.

"I know what he said. But we need to know their status and the ship's hull is interfering with their transmissions. We'll have to chance it."

Mitchey climbed higher so that we had a clear line-of-sight over the mountain ridge between us and the ship.

"Okay, Witch." I suddenly heard Dad's voice clearly. "When we open the hatch, they'll know who we are. Let's be sharp. I'll take lead."

We heard more sounds through our headsets, then what sounded like the airplane's access hatch being opened up.

"Hey, you're not Franklin," said an aggressive voice. "Where the hell is Franklin?"

"Franklin couldn't make it," I heard Dad say. "He had an unfortunate run in with an airplane prop. We came out instead. We have a federal search warrant for this ship. I'm Marshal Armstrong."

"A search warrant you say?" came the response. "We don't care about no stinking search warrant. Take 'em!"

Suddenly there was scuffling and fighting and yelling.

"Call the Coast Guard," said Mitchey.

"Cutter Resolute, this is Bay Watch. Do you copy? Over," I called, almost in a panic.

"This is Resolute. Go ahead Bay Watch," came the calm reply.

"Resolute, there's trouble on the *Finnlandia*. We think my dad and the colonel have been attacked."

"Bay Watch. We'll launch our helio in two minutes. It will be on site with an armed boarding party in thirty minutes."

"Can't you get here sooner?" I asked.

"Negative," came the response. "We are still about sixty-five miles out. But we'll get there as soon as we can, son."

"Roger, Resolute, thanks," I said, very dissatisfied that the cutter couldn't make better time.

"Resolute clear."

"Bay Watch clear."

I turned to look at Mitchey. Garbled transmissions were still coming over the radio. I was scared.

"We have to do *something*, now!" I shouted to Mitchey.

Suddenly Colonel Doctor's voice came over loud and clear.

"Andy, call Elmendorf! Tell them *x-ray one five* and your posit ..." I heard a 'whomp' sound and then the mike went dead.

"Mitchey!" I yelled. "They've been cut off!"

18
Flight to Shore

Mitchey pulled the airplane over into a steep bank and headed straight towards the ship.

"I'll try to divert their attention. Call the air base NOW!" shouted Mitchey.

I flipped the radio switches to the number two radio and keyed the mike.

"Elmendorf Operations. This is Cessna flight one eight five Alpha Juliet, code sign Bay Watch." I was surprised how calm my voice sounded. "Do you copy? We've got an emergency! Do you copy?"

"This is Elmendorf Ops. We read your weak transmission. Acknowledge your emergency. Say location and nature of the problem." I could hardly hear his voice.

"We're over Montague Bay. Colonel Doctor and my dad are in trouble on the *Finnlandia.* The colonel said to tell you x-ray one five. Repeat x-ray one five," I said.

"We confirm x-ray one five. Flight of two will arrive in under five minutes," said the controller.

"Huh? Did you say five minutes?" I asked. How could a flight from Elmendorf be here in five minutes? The base was over 120 miles away.

I couldn't understand the response. We had gotten too low to receive their radio transmissions.

We were about two miles from the ship and closing at 180 miles per hour, the max our bird could fly. As we closed on the *Finnlandia,* I could see people standing on the deck of the ship. There seemed to be a scuffle going on.

Mitchey pitched the plane down steeply and dived towards the ship, as if to ram it.

"What are you doing?" I yelled.

"Giving them a scare," she yelled back. "Maybe your Dad and the colonel can break free if we create a diversion."

As we rocketed towards the ship, people began running in different directions. I could just make out Dad and the colonel fighting with others. We zoomed close to the rear deck and past the ship's superstructure at high speed.

Mitchey started to pull the plane up, then yelled, "Andy! They're shooting at us!"

I looked off to my right and saw puffs of smoke coming from high up on the superstructure. Our airplane began to shake wildly.

"We've been hit!" she cried out. "Feels like they hit something in the tail."

She was trying to control the plane, but the controls were too heavy for her. We were descending rapidly toward the surface of the bay. Another five seconds, and we'd be history.

"Andy!" she shouted. "Grab the control wheel and help me pull it back."

I grabbed my wheel and pulled back on it with all my might. It would barely move.

"Pull hard!" Mitchey yelled desperately.

Suddenly I remembered something I'd read. I planted my feet firmly on the dashboard, and hauled back on the wheel as hard as I could, pushing with my feet for extra leverage.

It worked. The airplane began to come out of its dive toward the water. We must have missed the surface by only ten or fifteen feet. The plane was still shaking violently, but as we slowed down, the shaking subsided. We were climbing and were now about 200 feet above the water, headed for shore.

"Andy," said Mitchey. "I've lost control of my rudder pedals. The control cables to my pedals are not working. Let me get my feet up on the dash, then you see if your rudder pedals are working."

She got her feet up on the dash, and used all her strength to hold back on the wheel.

"Okay," she said, "try your pedals."

I took my feet off the dash. As I did so the nose dipped. I quickly put my feet back up and pulled on the wheel. The plane steadied, but was still shaking pretty good.

"What are we going to do, now?" I asked, realizing for the first time that I was really scared.

"We need some leverage to help hold back this control wheel while you try to get your feet on the rudder pedals. We need both the control wheel and the pedals to land this bird," she said.

She was looking around the cabin.

"Andy, where does your dad keep his tie-down ropes?" Mitchey asked.

"Way in the back," I replied.

"No good," she said.

"Of course!" she hollered suddenly. "Andy, in my survival bag under the seat are a set of ropes. When I tell you to, lean over and grab one of those ropes out of the bag. See that O-ring fastened to the ceiling behind me? That's an anchor for tying down cargo. Slip one end of the rope through the ring, then tie the other end around the control wheel. Got it?"

I got it. The rope would act like a pulley to give us the extra leverage we needed to control the damaged plane.

"Mitchey, I've got it. But can you hold the wheel back alone?"

The plane was shaking more violently, even though our airspeed had come down.

"Yes, if you move fast. Just hurry, Andy, because I don't think this baby is going to stay in the air a very long time.

"Are you ready?" she asked.

"Yes," I shouted.

"*Now!*" she yelled, and pulled hard on the control wheel.

I let go of my wheel, and the plane dipped. Mitchey strained and it came back up. I shoved my hand under her seat and grabbed the bag. I quickly found the ropes.

I turned to reach back to the O-ring, but my seat belt was too tight. I couldn't reach it.

I frantically unsnapped my belt. Leaning back over Mitchey, I slipped the rope through the ring.

"Quickly, Andy. Tie off one end to the control

wheel," Mitchey yelled. She was shaking from the physical strain of trying to hold the plane's nose up in the air.

I looped one end of the rope over the wheel and tied it off using two half hitches.

"What do I do with this other end?" I asked Mitchey.

"Loop that one over the control wheel, too, and tie it tight," she ordered.

"But how will you fly?" I asked.

"Just do it now!" she yelled. "Tie it *tight!*"

So I tied off the other end of the rope.

Mitchey let up on the control wheel. The plane came over to a level position, but didn't start descending. The rope was holding firm.

"Your controls are still functioning, I think," said Mitchey, as she rubbed her arms. "Check your rudder pedals."

I put my feet on the rudder pedals, and pushed on the left one. The plane started a turn to the left.

"That's enough!" she cried out. "Bring her back to a level position."

I pushed more gently on the other pedal. The plane came back to level flight.

"Now, Andy. You are going to land this plane," she said.

"*Me!*" I exclaimed.

"I can hold the back pressure on the wheel using this leverage system. You steer us to a landing using the rudder pedals, and the left and right movement of the control wheel. I'll do the power management, you fly the plane," she said.

Just then we shot over the beach at about 300 feet.

"I'm pulling back on the power." She pulled back the throttle control and the engine slowed down.

"We've got a good two miles of open beach," said Mitchey. "Try to land her in the area just between the soft sand and the surf. Okay, now turn to the left."

I nodded and gently turned the plane down the beach. We started to descend.

"I'll control the altitude with the throttle. You just keep her lined up. Remember, hold that back pressure and use your rudder pedals to hold the plane straight as we land," said Mitchey.

I was concentrating hard. As we neared the beach, a small gust of wind blew us off to the right. I thought for sure we were going to lose it.

"Ease her back, Andy!" said Mitchey. "Just a little rudder and keep the left wing low."

I complied. As we approached the landing, I tried

to remember what Dad always said. "Hold that stick back in your gut, and dance on the rudder pedals. Keep the nose pointed straight ahead and use the rudder pedals," he'd say. I tried to follow his advice.

Mitchey added power as we started to touch down on the sand.

"Power will help us on landing," she said. "Hold her steady."

We were on the ground and rolling to a stop. Just then, another gust of wind caught me off guard. The plane started to swerve away from the ocean. We were going into a ground loop. I didn't know what to do.

Mitchey pull back on the throttle, shut off the engine, and yelled, "Left rudder, Andy, *stomp* on that pedal!"

I held back on the wheel, and tried to do what she said. But I couldn't reach the pedal and turn the control wheel at the same time.

Mitchey saw what was happening. Quickly she grabbed her survival knife from her bag and severed the rope holding the wheel back. Then she dropped the knife and grabbed the wheel and turned the wheel to the left.

"*Stomp* on that pedal, now!" she yelled.

I stomped on the pedal and we were able to bring the plane under control. We slowed and rolled to a stop.

We were alive. And Dad's plane was okay. But Mitchey didn't even give me a moment to start breathing again.

"Andy, get out of the plane, now! There might be a fire!" she yelled.

We opened our doors and jumped out, Mitchey grabbing her survival bag as she went. We ran about 50 yards away from the damaged aircraft, and sat down in the sand.

"We made it!" I said. "We did it!"

Mitchey looked at me. She was tired but she smiled. "Andy, you were super. I couldn't have done it alone." Then she gave me a big hug.

I was elated at our luck. Then I thought of Dad and the colonel.

"What about Dad?" I asked Mitchey. We both looked toward the *Finnlandia* out in the bay.

Mitchey reached into her survival bag and pulled out a portable radio.

"I'll tune to the emergency frequency," she said. "Maybe we can pick up the Coast Guard." But the Coast Guard helicopter was still probably 25 minutes away and we couldn't raise them.

Then I remembered x-ray one five.

"Mitchey, do you think I heard the controller at Elmendorf right?" I asked. "That they'd have two planes here in five minutes?"

Mitchey was about to respond when two dark shapes appeared over the mouth of the bay. They were accelerating down from a high altitude. I could tell by the twin tails that they were Air Force F-15s. But what could they possibly do? They were flying way too fast.

They flew low over the ship and each pulled up into a steep climbing turn. As they came around on the ship again, they both slowed down. Mitchey and I couldn't believe our eyes! The jets began to hover over the ship, just like the Harrier jump jets I'd seen fly at air shows.

"But F-15s can't hover," I said. "Oh, yeah," I suddenly remembered. "I read an article about secret tests the Air Force was making on F-15s. They were reported to be testing vectored-thrust jet engines that would allow the planes to do amazing things in the air."

"Like hover?" asked Mitchey.

"Like hover," I said.

The sound of the aircraft was deafening, even from where we were sitting on the beach. But we could hear the pilots broadcasting a warning to the ship. The words came clearly over Mitchey's hand-held radio.

"*SS Finnlandia*. This is Captain Murdoch of the U.S. Air Force. You are ordered to surrender to the officers on board your ship. If you do not comply immediately, we will disable your ship."

Over the radio came the response from the ship. "This is the captain of the *Finnlandia*. If you touch us we will kill the hostages."

Hostages! Dad was still okay! I thought.

"You will not detain us and you will allow us to transit to international waters," said the *Finnlandia* captain. "Do *you* understand?"

One of the F-15s slowly rolled to the right, and flew a full circle ending up about a quarter of a mile behind the ship. A rocket leaped from its left wing, accelerated and hit the ship just below the water line near its rudder.

"I say again, *Finnlandia*. This is Captain Murdoch of the U.S. Air Force. You will surrender to the officers on your ship. If you harm one of them, we will blow your ship out of the water. We have orders to detain you. If you do not comply, we will attack your ship. You have ten seconds to respond."

The seconds ticked away. Just as the second F-15 began to dip its nose to fire again on the *Finnlandia*, I heard Dad's voice over the radio.

"Murdoch, this is Armstrong. Cease fire! The captain has surrendered!"

"Cowboy! You okay? How's the Witch?" said Murdoch.

"We've got things under control," said Dad. "Witch says to take up a low cap over the ship until the helio from the Coast Guard gets here."

"Understand the Witch is glad we made magic for him. Will take up a low orbit at 10,000 feet to wait for the Guard helio," said Murdoch.

Dad came back over the radio, "Murdoch, can you see my plane over on the beach? Andy and Mitchey were in it. I think it took a hit."

Murdoch's F-15 headed straight towards Mitchey and I. Mitchey thumbed the mike switch.

"Murdoch, this is Mitchey Peters. We're fine."

"Roger that, Mitchey. Do you need medical assistance?" Murdoch asked. The jet zoomed low over our heads. It was one of the best-looking jets I had ever seen. The sound was awesome.

"Negative. Andy and I are fine, but I'm afraid Armstrong's 185 will need some repairs to its tail section before it'll fly again," said Mitchey.

"Understand everyone's okay. Did you copy that, Cowboy?" said Murdoch.

"That's affirmative," said Dad. "Can you guys hear me?" he asked over his radio.

"We sure can," responded Mitchey.

"Thanks for the diversion. You really gave these creeps quite a scare. But, don't disobey orders, again!" Dad said.

I asked Mitchey for the hand-held.

"Dad," I said, "it was my fault. We were losing radio contact, and we knew you were in trouble. We had to try and help out somehow."

"Andy, I love you and you're the best kid in the whole world. Thanks for saving our lives. Don't worry, though. We'll have a talk about punishment later on." I heard him chuckle.

Mitchey and I looked at each other. She was relieved. But I wondered what Dad was thinking up for punishment.

19
Coast Guard Cutter Resolute

So what *is* x-ray one five?" I asked Colonel Doctor, after the Coast Guard helicopter had flown us to the Resolute, and we were gathered in the captain's lounge.

"Well, Andy," he said, "the x-ray one five is an experimental model of our F-15 Eagle single-seat fighter we've been testing here in Alaska. It's been modified to intercept drug traffickers. It detects ships off shore, hovers, and has an external communication system that lets us give orders to people on sea or land when we don't have radio contact. We've also modified some of the computer software so that the aircraft has better night detection capability. And, as you saw, it can hover using vectored thrust from its jet engines."

"How'd they get out to us so fast?" I asked.

"When your dad asked me to help him go after the *Finnlandia*, I ordered our two experimental aircraft to be ready to support us if we got into trouble. They were on alert, and already in the air when the controller at Elmendorf received your emergency call. It only took a few minutes at top speed to reach the Bay."

"That's some kind of flying," I said.

"Speaking of some kind of flying, pal," said Dad, "I'm very impressed that you and Mitchey were able to land the 185. That was quite a feat."

"If Andy hadn't put his feet up on the dash to give us the leverage to pull back on the control wheel, we'd be swimming with the salmon in the sound," said Mitchey, who was sitting next to Dad. "How'd you know to do that?" she asked, turning to me.

"I read a book last year about the MIG-17, an old Russian jet used in the Vietnam War. If the MIG exceeded 430 knots, the only way the pilot could regain control was to put his feet up on the dash and pull back on the control stick with all his might. Sometimes he succeeded. Sometimes he didn't. Anyway, I remembered that, and figured it was worth a try."

"Well, that was a superb move on your part, Andy.

You deserve a medal, as far as I'm concerned," said Colonel Doctor.

"I think you and Sam are the ones deserving medals—trying to arrest a ship full of criminals by yourselves," said Mitchey.

"Yeah," I said. "What happened out there?"

"They jumped us almost as soon as we were on board," said Dad. "We were pretty badly outnumbered. They didn't care that we were federal officers and carrying a federal warrant, or that the Coast Guard was on its way. They knew they were finished with their work and that they'd be in international waters before the cutter arrived. They just figured on tying us up and dropping us overboard. We were arguing with them about it when you and Mitchey came to the rescue. You can imagine we were pretty glad to have your "voice" in the argument. Even if you disobeyed orders." I squirmed when he said that.

"Did you find out what those guys were doing out there?" I asked the colonel.

"Mining, just like we thought. But not only the metal nodules," he said. "They found diamonds, too, and have been secretly strip mining the area for almost five weeks. We estimate they've hauled out more than $500 million worth of materials for their foreign sponsors."

"You know, Sam," said Mitchey, "I still can't figure out how those goons knew I was in Girdwood. How could they have figured out so quickly where my plane went down?"

"That had me puzzled too," said Dad. "But Witch discovered the answer on board the *Finnlandia*. Witch, why don't you explain."

"Turns out the ship had several radar- and video-equipped, remote-piloted drones. Basically, they're sophisticated radio-controlled model airplanes. They have wingspans of about 10 feet, and can stay aloft for over 24 hours. The military uses drones for recon. They're not too difficult to build or acquire, and they have a range of about 100 miles with the right relay equipment."

"Hey!" I exclaimed. "I remember that." Dad looked at me. "When Mr. Spernak was fixing Mitchey's plane up in the pass, I thought I heard a model plane a couple of times but didn't see anything. I didn't think much about it because it seemed like a weird place to be flying a model plane."

"It was a pretty good idea," said Colonel Doctor. "The ship's crew could easily launch and recover the drones. They launched one right after they saw Mitchey's plane fly just a little too close to their operation. Just suspicious, I guess. From then on they watched her everywhere she went. The video-tapes were on the ship."

Mitchey shivered. "Gives me the creeps to think I was being watched from the sky."

Dad looked at me and said, "Now, my little rule breaker, I wonder what would be an appropriate punishment, for not following my directions to stay out of harm's way."

I didn't like the direction this conversation was heading.

"Gee, Dad, I did save your life, you know." Everyone laughed.

"Yes, I'll take that information into account," he smiled.

"That old hanger you own could sure use a good cleaning," said the colonel.

"And your Super Cub is due for clean and wax job," said Mitchey.

I groaned. I hated waxing the wings. They're huge and my arms get really tired waxing the underside of them. This was going to be a very sore lesson.

"And when you're done with the hanger and the plane..." said Dad.

Oh great, I thought to myself, this wasn't over yet.

"...you'll start F.A.A. ground school. If you pass your written test, and demonstrate a broad knowledge of aviation, Mr. Spernak is going to give you flying lessons," he concluded.

"You're kidding!" I exclaimed.

"With your ability," said Mitchey with pride, "you should be piloting the Cub in no time."

I was going to learn to fly! It would be worth waxing the Cub.

"Congratulations, Andy. You really did a great job out there," Dad said. He looked out the porthole at Montague Bay then back at me. "You really are the best kid a dad could ever ask for. I love you, Bud," and with that Dad picked me up off the floor and gave me a big bear hug.

ORDER FORM

Name _____

Address _____

City/State/Zip _____

Phone _____

Enclosed is my check for $12.95 ($9.95 +$3 shipping & handling) for *SABOTAGE FLIGHT*.

DIMI PRESS
3820 Oak Hollow Lane, SE
Salem, OR 97302-4774

Phone 1-800-644-DIMI(3464) for orders
or 1-503-364-7698 for further information
or FAX to 1-503-364-9727
or by INTERNET to dickbook@aol.com

Call toll-free and order now!

OTHER DIMI PRESS PRODUCTS FOR YOU

TAPES are available for................................ $7.95 each

    #1-LIVE LONGER, RELAX
    #2-ACTIVE RELAXATION
    #3-CONQUER YOUR SHYNESS
    #4-CONQUER YOUR DEPRESSION
    #5-CONQUER YOUR FEARS
    #6-CONQUER YOUR INSOMNIA
    #7-CONQUER YOUR CANCER
    #8-LAST LONGER, ENJOY SEX MORE
    #9-WEIGHT CONTROL
    #10-STOP SMOKING
    #11-LIVE LONGER, RELAX (female voice)
    #12-ACTIVE RELAXATION (female voice)
    #13-UNWIND WHILE DRIVING
    #14-RELAX AWHILE
    #15-RELAX ON THE BEACH/MEADOW
    #16-HOW TO MEDITATE

TAPE ALBUM has six cassettes and is titled:

    GUIDE TO RELAXATION $29.95

BOOKS:

    HOW TO FIND THOSE HIDDEN JOBS gives tips
    on searching for a job..............................$13.95

    SURVIVING NATURAL DISASTERS is a guide to
    preparing for disasters.............................$14.95

    BUILD IT RIGHT! is a book of advice on what to
    watch out for as you build your own home...........$16.95

    FEEL BETTER! LIVE LONGER! RELAX is a manual
    of relaxation techniques & a history of relaxation.$9.95

    KOMODO, THE LIVING DRAGON (Rev. Ed.)is the
    only account of the world's largest lizard $14.95

    BLACK GLASS, a hardcover novel about a gay man in
    the Merchant Marine at the time of Vietnam $19.95